RAMPAGE

Also by Leslie Ernenwein
in Large Print:

Bullet Breed
Gunhawk Harvest
Trigger Justice

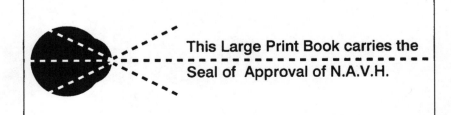

RAMPAGE

LESLIE ERNENWEIN

WHEELER
PUBLISHING

Published in 2004 by arrangement with
Golden West Literary Agency.

Wheeler Large Print Western.

The text of this Large Print edition is unabridged.
Other aspects of the book may vary from the original edition.

Set in 16 pt. Plantin by Al Chase.

Printed in the United States on permanent paper.

Library of Congress Cataloging-in-Publication Data

Ernenwein, Leslie.
    Rampage / Leslie Ernenwein.
      p. cm.
    ISBN 1-58724-716-X (lg. print : sc : alk. paper)
    1. Colorado River (Colo.-Mexico) — Fiction. 2. Large type
books. I. Title.
PS3555.R58R36 2004
  813´.54—dc22   2004042009

For

HARRY STERN

whose faith in Imperial Valley
stood the test of time.

As the Founder/CEO of NAVH, the only national health agency solely devoted to those who, although not totally blind, have an eye disease which could lead to serious visual impairment, I am pleased to recognize Thorndike Press★ as one of the leading publishers in the large print field.

Founded in 1954 in San Francisco to prepare large print textbooks for partially seeing children, NAVH became the pioneer and standard setting agency in the preparation of large type.

Today, those publishers who meet our standards carry the prestigious "Seal of Approval" indicating high quality large print. We are delighted that Thorndike Press is one of the publishers whose titles meet these standards. We are also pleased to recognize the significant contribution Thorndike Press is making in this important and growing field.

Lorraine H. Marchi, L.H.D.
Founder/CEO
NAVH

★ Thorndike Press encompasses the following imprints: Thorndike, Wheeler, Walker and Large Pr int Press.

AUTHOR'S NOTE:

Although this story is based on historic events that occurred during the early days of the Imperial Valley irrigation project, the selection and in some instances the continuity of events have been purposely adjusted to suit the needs of plot. All characters herein mentioned, with the exception of Epes Randolph, E. H. Harriman, Oliver Wozencraft, Jack Carrillo, F. H. Newell, and Milton Whitney, are fictional. If the name of any other actual person has been used, it is coincidental and was not included in the considerable amount of source material that furnished the basic ingredients of this story.

LESLIE ERNENWEIN
Tucson, Arizona
September 1953

CHAPTER ONE

The river was strong. Suckled by the watershed breasts of six states, it lunged into the long rock-walled slot of Grand Canyon with a violence that lifted racketing echoes against high ramparts. Sweeping southward, it flooded willow-fringed sloughs at the Gila's muddy mouth, carved new channels across sand bars, created islands that soon vanished. Then, converging and cresting, it roared beneath the railroad bridge at Yuma and hurled a monstrous wedge of silt-laden water through the wrecked intake gate at Pilot Knob, through a ruin of tilted piles and splintered planks and dissolving embankments.

Ben Roman, construction boss of Imperial Development, stood at the breached barrier's north end and said, "That goddamn river!"

The group of perspiring men who stood near Roman could not hear what he said; but now, as he flung a final sandbag into the thunderous cataract of chocolate-brown water, they understood his gesture of defiance. The river was an old antagonist; a foe he fought and hated and respected.

One of the men stepped close to Roman

and shouted, "The Red Bull has beat us again!"

Roman shrugged. Ancient sweat stains darkened the band of his flat-crowned Texas hat. Fatigue was a dullness in his eyes. He said, "I'll go warn the settlers."

As he turned toward camp, a cynical smile altered his high-boned cheeks and he added, "They'll hate my guts."

There had been no rain here for months, yet a mile-wide strip of mud curved across the flats east of Deseronto. The sun-cracked parchment of crusting mud made a broad brown mark upon the tawny land, an umber smear running on and on until it merged with the metallic shimmer of far desert. There was a message in the mud. It told of wrecked control gates and breached levees and ruined crops to the south, where flood-waters had struck their first and hardest blows; it formed a pattern of premonition to the mind of Ben Roman, who now rode a weary horse into town.

This was August 1905. Noon's shadowless sun scorched the tents and tin-roofed shacks and rutted dust of Deseronto. Here, in the wagon yard behind a barrack-like building marked "Imperial Development Company," Ben Roman dismounted. A three-day growth of black whiskers shagged his angular face, tallying the time he'd been asaddle, and trail dust lay like a ragged shawl on his shoulders. For nearly four years Ben Roman had coaxed and cursed a small army of men into constructing an irrigation canal across the southern desert, a fabulous project that the newspapers referred to as "John Chilton's dream." During the past three days he had witnessed the destruction of that dream.

Dirty and dog-tired and slow-moving, Roman uncinched his saddle. He was lifting it from the bay gelding's wet back when Mohee Jim Brimberry came out of the barn.

"How's things look betwixt here and the big ditch?" Brimberry inquired.

"God-awful," Roman said. He hung his saddle on a peg inside the doorway and then led his horse over to the watering trough. "It could've been worse," he said, nodding toward the mud strip. "Didn't miss town by much."

"Scairt hell out of the store folks," Brimberry said. "They toted sandbags out there, figurin' the flood might wash this whole shebang away. Oscar Hoffman was fidgety as a sack of snakes for fear his mercantile stock would get wet."

Roman drank cheek to cheek with his horse.

"The Citizens' Committee called on John Chilton last night, wantin' to know why he couldn't control the Colorado," Brimberry said. He grinned and spat tobacco juice into

11

the dust and wiped his sorrel mustache on the back of a big-knuckled hand. "You'd of thought Chilton was God, the way they talked."

The thought came to Ben Roman that folks couldn't be blamed for thinking John Chilton could play God with the river. They had seen him divert the Colorado's south-flowing water into an irrigation canal that flowed northward in seeming opposition to the law of gravity. Other men had dreamed of doing it; men like Oliver Wozencraft, who'd first discovered the possibility in 1849. But only John Chilton had hurdled the high barriers of doubt.

"Clark Hazelhurst is complainin' about his settlers bein' washed out," Brimberry said, as if relishing this recital of bad news. "Several of 'em told Hazelhurst they was goin' to sue the company for all the damage the flood done their places. From reports that's come in, I reckon there'll be more goddamn lawsuits than you could shake a stick at."

"Shouldn't wonder," Roman said. He took the horse into a stall and forked it a feed of hay. "Did MacIvor get back from Pilot Knob?"

"Nope." Mohee chuckled, and spat again. "Maybe Mac took one look at what happened to his intake gate and decided to quit the country. Them settlers ain't goin' to feel friendly toward our chief engineer. They ain't likin' what happened to their crops."

While Roman dipped a measure of oats from the grain bin, Mohee Jim asked, "You reckon the company will go broke now, sure enough?"

Roman shrugged and, guessing what was in this gun toting Texan's mind, said flatly, "Nobody's forcing you to stay, Mohee. You're free to drift any time you like."

"Sure," Brimberry said, "and so be you. Chilton never done us no favors that I know of. It's the other way around. We sweated out his surveyin' deal when a Cocopah Injun wouldn't of took the hellish heat. Then we stayed on to build his drunkard's dream of a canal. I say you done enough, Ben. There's better ways of earnin' your frijoles than bein' construction boss of a broken-down irrigation outfit." He peered soberly at Roman now; he said, "It's aged you somethin' awful. You look six years older'n God."

"Which is how I feel," Roman admitted.

Brimberry followed him to the doorway. "It ain't like you didn't have nothin' else to do. My scheme for a wild-horse gather in the Mogollones might make us rich. And think how purely elegant it would be up there out of this stinkin' heat. All we got to do is get a pack outfit together and rim them ridges while the weather's right for it. Come November, we'd have us more mustangs corralled than we could count."

13

Roman unstrapped his spurs and hung them on the saddle horn. "You run off at the mouth like a swivel-jawed land agent," he said. "You put me in mind of Clark Hazelhurst."

"But why should we wear ourselves down to nubbins for a bunch of sod-bustin' settlers?" Brimberry demanded. "It ain't no meat off'n our rump what happens to 'em."

"Who said it was?" Roman asked irritably. Roosting on a grain bin, he took out his Durham sack and fashioned a cigarette. "How's John taking the bad news?"

"Like always. By God, you'd think his life depended on irrigatin' this damned desert."

"Maybe it does," Roman mused, thumbing a match to flame. "It's cost John everything he had, including a wife."

"He must be loco in the head," Mohee Jim scoffed. "Why any man would let a goddamn desert come betwixt him and a sweet-smellin' blonde wife is beyond me. It just don't make sense. Hell, there's a time for deserts and such when a man gets past his needin's. The time for women is when he's in his prime."

"Suppose," Ben Roman said.

It occurred to him now that he had worked with this gangling rawboned man for five years without knowing what was inside him. For all of his being a free talker, Mohee Jim hadn't told much about himself. Why, for instance, did he always wear a gun? Brimberry

14

had hired out originally as a packer on the surveying project, and afterward was put in charge of the team stock. It wasn't unusual for a man to pack a gun, but Brimberry's .45 was as much a part of his garb as the galluses that supported his bachelor-patched pants.

Casually now Roman said, "I've never seen you without a gun strapped on, Mohee. Seems odd."

"Nothin' odd about it, if you knowed the story."

"Secret?"

"Why, no. Not exactly."

A grin creased Brimberry's russet cheeks. He eased down on his heels and propped his back against a stall partition. "It started in Texas a tol'able time ago," he began, then ceased speaking as Clark Hazelhurst came into the barn.

Imperial's land agent peered at Roman and said, "You look like you'd been up in the brush with a Cocopah squaw."

There were those who said this bland-faced promoter could smile a man out of his right senses. But Ben Roman didn't like him, and showed it in the way he said, "I don't get paid for looking pretty."

Hazelhurst winked at Mohee Jim. He said, "Ben feels like he looks."

"My business and none of yours," Roman muttered.

15

"Of course," Hazelhurst agreed good-naturedly. "But Chilton is real anxious to see you, Ben. He's convinced that the settlers are claiming more damage than was done. He thinks your report will prove him right."

"Damage stories seldom lose anything in the telling," Roman said. "Never knew a sodbuster to belittle his troubles."

"But they're not exaggerating," Hazelhurst insisted. "I drove through some of that flooded area yesterday and saw the damage with my own eyes."

"And damn near foundered a good team doin' it," Brimberry complained.

Ignoring that criticism, Hazelhurst said, "I'm taking the afternoon train west. I'm going to tell the board of directors what I think of a development company that brings in settlers and then floods them out with makeshift control gates and inadequate levees."

"Your privilege," Roman said. He gave Hazelhurst a narrow-eyed regard, remembering that this man had been hired by the Los Angeles office.

Roman flipped his cigarette out the doorway and looked Hazelhurst in the eye and said, "Be damn sure you don't hang the blame on John Chilton."

"Sounds like a warning," Hazelhurst said.

"It is," Roman said. "A warning from me to you. John has lost enough. I'll not see him rawhided out of his job, which is all he has left."

Hostility altered Hazelhurst's face, tightening the muscles of his cheeks and compressing the fullness from his lips. He was about Roman's age, a few inches shorter and several pounds heavier — a yellow-haired, handsome man with a pronounced cleft in his chin. He said, "I resent your warning."

"Figured you would."

It was a challenge, plain enough to rouse Mohee Jim, who got up and watched with tight expectancy as these two eyed each other in the muscle-cocked way of dogs with raised hackles.

"You've got no right to warn me about a thing like that," Hazelhurst complained. Yet even now, with anger having its way with him, his voice held a smooth civility.

"To hell with talk," Roman muttered.

Hazelhurst shook his head, and now the bland smile came back to his face. He said, "You're cranky tired, Ben. You need some sleep."

He went out into the sun-hammered yard.

"All paw and beller," Mohee Jim said disgustedly. "Never saw a man who could talk so big with so little sand in his craw. You know what he's been tellin' around? I heard him spout off to Slim Lacey at supper last night. He told her the settlers might get so worked up they'd lynch him on account of the promises he made 'em. Now, ain't that somethin' to fret about?"

"It's an idea," Roman said, his haggard face showing a cynical amusement. "Guess I'll go try a cup of Slim's coffee, then give John the bad news."

"Don't you want to hear the story about what happened to me in Texas?"

"Some other time." Glancing at the doorway thermometer, Roman loosed a low whistle. "Hundred and eleven in the shade."

"Sure, and gettin' hotter every day," Brimberry called after him. "Think on what I said about the wild-horse gather, Ben. Think on it."

Roman nodded and walked across the wagon yard, choosing a route that would take him to Main Street without passing John Chilton's office. There had been other times when he had dreaded to face Chilton, but none so bad as now. John had been so sure the new intake gate would hold against flash floods, so serenely confident that the long fight was won at last. Roman frowned, knowing how it would be with Chilton; and because a sense of futility had nagged him for the past three days, he thought: Maybe Mohee Jim is right.

Main Street's plank walks were deserted. One man worked with hammer and saw constructing a veranda railing at the new Empire Hotel. A settler's team stood in droop-headed

18

patience at the Mercantile loading platform, and two saddled horses were tied to the hitch rack in front of Lew Gallatin's tent saloon.

Swede Erickson, standing in the doorway of his alley blacksmith shop, called, "Is the damage as bad as they tell it?"

"Bad enough," Roman said, not stopping to talk.

Heat radiated from the street's hoof-pocked dust; it sucked moisture from his sweat-dampened shirt, leaving salt-rime stains at the armpits. Again, as he had many times, Roman marveled that men had set up business establishments in this sun-punished place, and that a woman should share such perverse notions. Especially a young, good-looking woman like Slim Lacey, who had opened the town's only restaurant. He had known her for six months, a dark-haired girl of twenty-four with hazel eyes and long legs that made her appear taller than she was. Slim seldom complained about the heat or seemed to mind the primitive conditions; yet she was no gushy optimist parroting Clark Hazelhurst's brags about the Valley's future.

Entering the boxy little restaurant, Roman remembered what he had thought the first time he saw Slim Lacey. All woman, he'd told himself, and that's how she looked now, standing there behind the counter with rolled-up sleeves revealing the soft contours of her arms, and a snug-fitting apron empha-

19

sizing the swell of her breasts.

Roman peered in mock wonderment, rubbing his bloodshot eyes as if dazzled by the sight of her. "Are you the woman I heard about?" he inquired. "The one they call Big Slim?"

Her eyes retained their attentive serenity. She gave him a leisurely appraisal, as if sizing up an offensive stranger. "You look awful," she said, not smiling.

Roman thumbed his jaw in the whimsical fashion of a man reluctantly admitting the need for a shave.

"I don't mean the brush," she said. "It's your eyes. They look like burned holes in a blanket. Haven't you slept since you left town?"

"Nary a wink," Roman admitted.

"And you're the one who doesn't care what happens to a bunch of fool settlers," she scoffed.

"I don't," Roman said, and climbed onto a stool.

Slim poured him a cup of coffee, moving with an effortless ease that was neither hurried nor hesitant. "Roast beef or steak?"

"Beef," Roman said, and watched her walk toward the kitchen lean-to. Her hair, drawn back and fashioned in a bun, was dark brown against the ivory nape of her neck.

When Slim came back from the kitchen with a well-filled plate, Roman asked,

"Where's your dad?"

"Taking his afternoon siesta. This heat gets him down. He wants me to sell out and go to the coast."

That surprised Roman. Joe Lacey's optimistic predictions for the future had excelled even those of Clark Hazelhurst; he'd been Deseronto's leading booster. "Did the flood change him that much?"

"It's not the flood, and he hasn't changed."

Slim made an open-palmed gesture of futility. "Dad was born fiddle-footed. Any place looks good to him until he lives in it for six months. Then he wants to try somewhere else. But I'm through following him around. He's going to stay put this time or go by himself."

"Good," Roman said. "Maybe you'll be needing a partner."

"You?"

Roman nodded.

She laughed at him. "Bachelors are no better than widowers when it comes to staying put."

"Maybe I wouldn't be a bachelor," Roman said.

Slim met his gaze directly: she said, "My mother married a fiddle-footed man and died in a cheap hotel. I'll never make that mistake."

"Not even for me?" Roman asked in mock chagrin.

Slim shook her head. "You'd always be traipsing off to see what's over the hill. Mohee Jim seems to think you'll go on mustang roundup with him."

"Just wishful thinking," Roman said.

Slim leaned on the counter and watched him eat. She studied his face as if seeking the answer to an old and perplexing question; as if not quite sure of what she saw, and wanting to be sure.

"You counting my whiskers?" Roman asked, giving her a kindred appraisal.

"Just thinking," Slim said.

"Wishful?"

She shrugged. "A man has to make a stand somewhere. He can't just keep drifting from place to place all his life."

"Some do," Roman said. "Some men are free as a ridge-running stud."

"And they turn into shiftless tramps," Slim said with more vehemence in her low voice than he'd heard before. "A man shouldn't spend his whole life trying to run away from himself." She nodded toward the lean-to living quarters. "That's Dad's trouble. He resents being a medium-sized toad in a small puddle. He thinks he could be a big toad if he found a better puddle."

The screen door creaked open now, and Roman turned to see George Frayne, Imperial's chief clerk.

"Mr. Chilton wants to see you," Frayne announced. "He's quite anxious to hear your report."

Roman grimaced. "Why does bad news always have to be rushed?" he demanded.

The bald, pursy-lipped clerk considered that question with the gravity of a man making a momentous decision. "I suppose it's because bad news is usually important," he suggested. "Take a death, for instance. There are funeral arrangements to be made, property settlements and outstanding accounts to be taken care of — perhaps a will to be probated."

Roman took out his Durham sack and fashioned a cigarette; he said, "I'll be over after a while."

"But Mr. Chilton is quite impatient to see you," Frayne said.

"I said I'd come, didn't I?" Roman said irritably. "You want it in writing?"

Plainly offended, Frayne backed to the doorway. "I merely wanted you to know how urgent it is," he explained on his way out.

"There," Roman muttered, "goes a pencil with ears." Seeing the suppressed amusement in Slim's eyes, he said, "George means well, I suppose. But he's always so sure he's doing the right thing."

"A common trait in men," Slim said.

Presently, as he paid for the meal, she asked, "Can your canal be repaired in time to save what crops weren't flooded out?"

"Maybe."

"But you don't think so?"

"I don't know," Roman admitted. "And if it wasn't for John Chilton I wouldn't give a damn." Then he grinned and patted her arm and said, "One thing I'm sure of, though."

"What?"

Roman turned to the screen door and opened it before saying, "You've got nice eyes, Slim — the nicest eyes I've ever seen."

Afterward, walking toward Imperial's office building, he wondered why Slim hadn't smiled or spoken while she watched him leave. Women, he'd thought, ran pretty much to a pattern, especially the young, warm-blooded ones. They might use different methods and alter the rules as they went along, but they played the same game for the same purpose: to attract male attention.

As Roman passed the Weekly Clarion office, Frank Monroe came to the doorway and asked, "How long do you think it will take to repair the levee and build a new intake gate?"

"Are you going to quote me in your newspaper?" Roman inquired.

"Of course."

Roman grinned at him. He said, "I'm no good at guessing," and walked on.

CHAPTER TWO

John Chilton, general manager in charge of field operations, hunched over a desk littered with reports of the Colorado's worst rampage since Imperial had dug its Alamo diversion canal. A small, meek-eyed man with a wispy saddle of graying hair, Chilton looked up now as Ben Roman came into the office. He took off his glasses and asked, "How bad is it, Ben?"

"Bad."

Chilton frowned as if in scholarly meditation. "I can't comprehend it," he said, poking at the papers. "How could the river have done so much damage in so short a time?"

Ben Roman sat down. He propped his boots on the desk rim and tilted back so that his long lean-shanked body was almost horizontal. "That's a lot of river, John."

"But these reports must be exaggerated," Chilton insisted. "The estimates are too high, aren't they, Ben?"

"Reckon not."

It was a sobering thing to see the hope fade from Chilton's eyes. He had been waiting for an accounting that would shrink the dimension of destruction. Refusing to accept the reports in their entirety, or Hazelhurst's verification of them, he had clung to a fragile strand of hope that now was broken. It made Ben Roman feel disloyal, as if he were failing a friend in need. But propping Chilton's false hopes wouldn't remedy the situation, so he said now, "I counted eleven breaks. Those levees could've been so much sawdust, the way that flash flood sifted through 'em." He contemplated Chilton through half-closed eyes for a long moment before asking, "Still think the Red Bull can be tamed?"

"Of course I do," Chilton said.

He got up and walked to the doorway and gazed out across the sun-baked town. "We've already built one monument to Oliver Wozencraft's dream, and there'll be others. This will be a metropolis some day, Ben — a great city sprouted from the seed planted in a surveyor's tent." A wishful smile brightened Chilton's brown eyes as he asked, "Remember how it was here six short years ago? Just sand and greasewood fifty horseback miles east of the San Jacintos and half as far west of Yuma. That's how we calculated its location, with nothing else to go by. Now it's a town, with a hotel and stores and a school. Why, we even have a weekly newspaper."

"Also a saloon and a brothel," Roman said slyly. "Don't forget them, John. They're a sure sign of progress."

26

Flies buzzed about an olla suspended from a rafter, and the clickety-clack of a typewriter came through the board partition. A picture of Chilton's ex-wife hung on the side wall, a large, lifelike photograph in an oval frame. Dust and flyspecks had dulled the gilt frame, but the glass was kept spotless by this little man who prized the memory of a woman he had loved and lost; a young, golden woman whose eyes had once been warm for him.

"I would have wagered anything that the intake gate was adequate," Chilton muttered. "Our calculations were based on exact measurements of every known variation in the current and action of the river."

Roman yawned and closed his eyes, slack-muscled now as a man could be. Presently he said, "Reckon I'll go take a bath. Haven't had my clothes off for three days."

But he made no move to get up.

Chilton came back to the desk and asked, "Did you see any sign of MacIvor's rig?"

"Saw some dust east a ways. Might be him." Roman took off his hat and fanned his perspiring face. "Guess I'll go take that bath, John."

"Well, I'd like for you to be here when MacIvor reports," Chilton said. "I'll need your moral support. Angus is the best chief engineer in the country, but he's a perfectionist, poor soul. He can't abide makeshifts, which is about all we have left to work with."

"All we've ever had," Roman said. "This outfit reminds me of a greasy-sack cowman I knew in Texas. Always an hour late and a dollar short." Then he asked, "Is the company still solvent?"

Chilton picked up a ledger sheet and glanced at its neat column of figures. "There's enough cash on hand for payrolls and some incidentals, but none for new equipment. I'm hoping the board of directors will induce Southern Pacific to come in with us. That's our one real hope, Ben."

"A poor hope," Roman said. "The Harrimans don't invest cash in a pipe dream. That's all this project is, until we lick the river. And maybe we won't lick it with makeshifts."

George Frayne opened an inner door and announced, "There's a man looking for Doc Shumway. Says his wife is having labor pains. Doc isn't in his office."

"Look for him at the hotel," Chilton suggested.

But Roman said, "Try the saloon, George. That's where you'll find him."

And when Frayne had gone back into the general office, Roman said, "Another sorry makeshift, John. You should've fired Shumway six months ago. He's a counterfeit if ever I saw one."

"I know," Chilton admitted. "The Los Angeles office is attempting to replace him. But doctors are hard to find."

Then, as a burly, red-faced man appeared in the doorway, Chilton exclaimed, "Come in, Angus! Come in and rest yourself. You look on the verge of sunstroke."

"I am," the chief engineer said. "A man must be daft to stay here in August." He dropped wearily into a chair and mopped his flushed, frown-rutted face with a bandanna. "The reports were right about what happened at Pilot Knob. That damned river just won't stay put, no matter what we do."

Ben Roman watched these two men and marveled that they should have become so closely associated, for they were unlike in almost every way. Chilton's optimism, which had impoverished him beyond hope of financial recovery, seemed to bounce with each blow of adversity. But Angus MacIvor was weighted by a scientist's calculating mind, and possessed no such buoyancy; doubting the project's soundness from the beginning, he had become more pessimistic with each reversal.

"Just how bad is it?" Chilton inquired.

"Completely wrecked," MacIvor said. "The intake gate has been ripped open for nearly two hundred feet. The first four miles of main canal are silted so high there is no diversion, now that the river has dropped to nearly normal. In other words, we're sunk, sanded, and finished."

Unabashed by that recital of ruin, Chilton asked serenely, "How long will it take us to repair the damage?"

"Longer than I care to contemplate. Longer than the settlers can survive without water."

Chilton's smile gave his eyes a curious youthfulness. "We'll manage somehow," he said.

"Somehow!" MacIvor shouted, his voice shrill with derision. He pounded the desk with a freckled fist. He demanded, "Have you no sense, man? Can't you understand that old Wozencraft was a witless dreamer seeing a mirage? The Reclamation Service survey has been proved correct. It said we were faced by insurmountable obstacles, and so we are!"

Chilton winced. He clasped his fragile hands in a nervous gesture and turned to Roman. "What do you say?" he asked hopefully.

Ben Roman focused his eyes on the scuffed toes of his boots. This, he realized, should be the showdown; an end of futile fighting against the river. If he agreed with MacIvor, the vote would stand two to one against John Chilton. The company directors were already skeptical of their general manager; they would probably accept a joint opinion from the chief engineer and superintendent of construction.

"I'd say Angus is correct, on paper," Roman said finally. "But I'm remembering what my old pappy said after the winter of the Big Die in Texas."

"What in God's name has that to do with a flood-busted irrigation project?" MacIvor demanded. "We're facing drought, not blizzards!"

Roman grinned at him. Mac wasn't a bad fellow, in his way. A trifle arrogant, and intolerant of any opinion that opposed his own. But there was no meanness in him. "Damned if I wouldn't welcome a good blizzard right now," Roman mused, and wiped his sweat-greased face on a hunched shoulder. "I've seen my share of hot weather, man and boy. But none like this. When I stopped by Gus Elmendorf's place this morning, his wife told me her setting hen hatched a dozen chickens in three days."

"What did your daddy say in Texas?" John Chilton prompted.

"Why, he said no man was ever licked until he quit."

"Exactly!" Chilton agreed, smiling his gratitude. "We can dredge the intake, narrow the channel with brush jetties, and —"

"The dredger is broke down," MacIvor interrupted. "By the time it could be fixed and dragged to Pilot Knob, there'd be enough damage suits to finish bankrupting the company."

31

Chilton turned again to Roman. "How long will it take to repair and move the dredger?"

"Upwards of three weeks. Maybe longer."

"Then we'll dig out the channel with fresnos, or by hand," Chilton decided.

"And what will you use for men?" MacIvor asked. "There's only a dozen of the construction crew left, and the settlers are working day and night to dig out their sanded laterals. You'll get no help from them."

Ben Roman lowered his boots from the desk rim. He took out his Durham sack and fashioned a cigarette with deliberate slowness while MacIvor predicted, "It would take that small a crew six months to do the job."

"Suppose I rounded up thirty or forty men in a week's time," Roman suggested.

"Where would you find that many lunatics who'd come to this hellhole in August? And supposing you should get them. Supposing we repair the intake and clean out the channel. What happens when the next flash flood comes roaring down that goddamn river?"

He waited for an answer. When it didn't come, he said, "I'll tell you what'll happen. Out go our brush jetties, out go our levees, and in comes the silt. If we had the financial backing to build a concrete gate, I'd say there was a chance. But we haven't got it, and we'll never get it."

"The company is trying to make a deal with Southern Pacific right now," Chilton announced. "If it goes through, we'll have the necessary equipment to construct a proper gate."

"If!" MacIvor shouted. "If!"

"An iffy deal, for a fact," Roman admitted. "But so is life. If your pappy hadn't met your mammy, you wouldn't be here, Angus."

There was no alteration in MacIvor's craggy face. "I say we're licked, by God! Licked!"

Again, as he had so many times, John Chilton rejected surrender. "We cannot stop now," he insisted. "Think how far we've come, Angus. Think of all we've accomplished. Four hundred miles of canals and laterals built. A hundred thousand acres of desert turned into tillable soil. And, despite the Agriculture Department's stupid pamphlet warning folks away, we've attracted upwards of two thousand settlers."

"Right," MacIvor said. "And it's those same settlers who'll skin us alive when we fail to furnish them the water Clark Hazelhurst promised in his advertisements." He grimaced, as if already plagued by a threat of mob violence. "They'll sue the company, but we're the ones they'll use their fists on. Or their ropes."

Ben Roman sat loosely relaxed, listening to the talk and thinking that MacIvor was right about the futility of battling the river. Long ago the Mexicans had named it El Toro Rojo — the Red Bull — because of annual rampages that flooded the delta land and sent silt-laden water rolling to the Salton Sink. Unpredictable as a wild bull was the Colorado; a docile conformist of months, it would lunge without warning in swift and wrathful rebellion.

MacIvor's pessimism was founded on fact. He had put all his engineering skill into devising an intake gate that would divert and control the river's water. But the Red Bull made a mockery of his best efforts. In one hour the flood-swollen Colorado ripped through the work of weeks, canceled months of preparations, ruined growing crops.

Judged on past performance, MacIvor's dour prediction of failure was wholly reasonable, while Chilton's faith seemed almost childish in its simplicity. What Mohee Jim called a "drunkard's dream of a canal" had become a nightmare of repetitious failure. But there was in Ben Roman a deep-rooted admiration for the little man who dedicated himself to a dream, whose mild eyes envisioned this vast desert transformed into a garden spot for hundreds of families.

Ranch-raised and rebel-bred, Roman had a horseman's disdain for land-hungry farmers swarming west with their toil-worn women and sniveling youngsters. The dream meant nothing to Ben Roman. His allegiance was to the dreamer.

"Give it one more try," he suggested. "I'll take the night train east with Mohee Jim. We'll be back inside of a week with upwards of forty men."

"How?" MacIvor demanded. "How will you get them?"

"One way or another," Roman said, and walked over to the doorway.

"A wild-goose chase if ever I saw one," MacIvor said. "You'll never get men to come here in August."

Roman took a long drag on his cigarette before asking, "Want to make a little bet?"

Angus MacIvor was no part of a gambler, but this opportunity to best a witless optimist tempted him. "I don't hold with wagering as a practice," he said. "However, I'll risk ten dollars that you don't get more than ten men."

"Make it fifty dollars and raise the head count to thirty men," Roman suggested.

MacIvor blinked. "Fifty dollars?" he asked, as if mentally squeezing each silver cartwheel.

Roman nodded, and now a new thought came to him. "I'll make you a better proposition," he offered. "One that can't cost you a penny. If we don't bring back thirty men within a week, I'll pay you fifty dollars. But if we do bring them, you promise to remain on the job six months, no matter what happens."

35

"Suppose another flash flood washes us out?"

"You stay on the job with John and me, regardless of consequences."

MacIvor thought it over. Finally he said, "You're on, and I'll collect my fifty a week from today."

Shrugging off that prediction, Roman turned to Chilton, whose scholarly face now wore a contented smile. "I'll need some cash for expenses, John."

"Of course," Chilton agreed. "Frayne will fetch it to your quarters within the hour."

Roman tipped his hat to Angus MacIvor. He licked his heat-flaked lips and grinned and said, "Six months on the job, come hell or high water."

When he walked out to the street John Chilton said, "I don't know how Ben will get those men, but he'll get them."

"I'll wager you ten dollars that he doesn't," MacIvor said.

Chilton shook his head. "I never gamble."

MacIvor peered at him, remembering how this little man had risked his personal fortune on an irrigation project, and lost it, along with a wife who refused to play second fiddle to a dream. The chief engineer was not noted for his sense of humor, but now chuckling amusement gripped him.

"So you never gamble!" he blurted, and loosed a hoot of sardonic laughter.

Slim Lacey watched her father pack a battered valise. He had awakened from his nap to tell her of a dream about a fabulous opportunity in Oregon. Reciting the fragmentary details had whetted his desire for travel until it was overwhelming. "I'll catch the afternoon train west," he decided. "By the time you sell this fly trap, I'll have a nice place all set for us in Oregon!"

As she watched him now, it was difficult for Slim to realize that her father was almost sixty years old. He was like an eager young man preparing for a vacation trip. His chubby, clean-shaven face was unlined, for he had never been one to worry. Even though his hair was thin on top and gray at the temples, his eyes were bright and lively as he said, "Don't hold out for a high price, daughter. Take what you can get, then come arunning. Oregon is a grand place."

Slim recalled that he had said the same thing about Texas and Arizona and California. Everyplace was grand until he'd spent a few months there. It would be the same in Oregon.

"I'll not be going there," she said, taking a cooky jar from a shelf and dumping its contents on the counter. There were half a dozen gold pieces among the bills and silver dollars; upwards to two hundred dollars all told.

"But why not?" Joe Lacey demanded.

Slim shrugged, put fifty dollars back into the jar, and placed it on the shelf.

"Why should you stay in this hot place?" Joe Lacey insisted.

"I'm tired of traipsing from one town to another," Slim said. "I'm tired of cheap hotels. This is the nearest thing to home I've had since I was a little girl."

Joe Lacey had taken out his leather money pouch and was opening its drawstrings; now he looked at her with more gravity in his eyes than Slim had ever seen there before. "It hasn't been good for you, has it," he said regretfully, "all this traveling from pillar to post?"

In this moment he looked old and tired and somehow pitiful to Slim. It was as if he saw himself for what he was, and had no excuses to offer for the wasted years.

Slim reached out and patted his arm. She smiled and said, "We've had good times, Dad. Lots of them. More good times than most people ever have."

That pleased him. It drove the gravity and regret out of him. "So we have," he agreed, and scooped the cash into his pouch without counting it.

Slim smiled, thinking that he had never fretted about money. And presently, as she walked with him to the depot, it seemed right that he should be going away. For him, life was a continuous adventure and change was its essence. His eyes were gay, almost boyish, as he said good-by to Frank Monroe and Swede Erickson and other men they met on the street. He even seemed to like Deseronto better, now that he was leaving it. To Clark Hazelhurst, who was also taking the train, Joe said, "This isn't a bad place to spend the winter. Perhaps I'll come back when they turn off the heat next October."

"But I thought you were sold on the Valley's future," Hazelhurst said. Turning to Slim, he asked, "Are you going to run out on us too?"

"Not me," Slim assured him. "I'm here to stay."

"Good. Just so you don't leave." His smile was like a caress, intimate as a kiss. "Don't you accept Frank Monroe's proposal while I'm away," he said, and got onto the train.

"Is Frank the reason you want to stay here?" her father asked.

When Slim shook her head, he counseled, "Don't ever marry a man who doesn't know how to laugh once in a while."

Slim nodded. As the conductor called, "All aboard," she put her arms around her father and whispered, "Perhaps I'll marry a real good-natured man like you."

Joe Lacey chuckled. He hugged her tight and kissed her and said, "Be a good girl, honey."

Slim nodded, keeping back the tears until he had climbed into the vestibule.

CHAPTER THREE

Refreshed by a bath, a shave, and five hours of dreamless sleep, Ben Roman boarded the nine-o'clock eastbound train with Jim Brimberry. At Yuma he held a brief consultation with the railroad's special officer. As the train pulled out he called, "Don't forget. Number Six on Friday."

Mohee Jim wondered about that. Ben had said they were on a labor-recruiting expedition to Tucson, but hadn't gone into details. And because any excuse to leave Deseronto was sufficient for Brimberry, he hadn't asked questions. But when Roman held a similar conversation with the special agent at Gila Bend and again warned about Number Six, Mohee's curiosity was aroused.

"What's all this about?" he inquired.

"A wager with Angus MacIvor."

Brimberry snorted. "You mean that tight-fisted galoot made a bet with money?"

"Something more valuable, Mohee. His presence on the job for six months, if I can gather a crew of thirty laborers."

"What's that got to do with these railroad cops?"

"They're my employment agents. They'll

round up vags and short-termers for me at three dollars a head, and have them ready to board Number Six when we come back through here on Friday."

Mohee Jim thought about that for upwards of five minutes while Ben Roman stretched out with his feet propped on the double seat. Finally Mohee Jim said, "Sounds like a shanghai deal to me, same as them ship captains worked on the Barbary Coast when they was short of sailors."

"Somewhat similar," Roman admitted.

"Well, supposin' them vags and jailbirds decide they want to leave the train before we get to Deseronto?"

"That's why I brought you," Roman said, and glanced at Brimberry's holstered gun. "What was that story you started to tell me about Texas?"

"It's a yarn I wouldn't want overheard," Brimberry said.

He looked at the sleeping passenger across the aisle, then gave the smoker's rear seats a deliberate appraisal. "Might be some kinfolk of Red Gillum, the man I killed in Texas."

"How'd it happen?" Roman prompted.

"Well, Gillum was like George Frayne in one respect. Couldn't stand to be wrong about anything. It must be awful havin' to be right all the time. Seems odd that a man should tote such a load by choice, but plenty

41

of 'em do. They just got to be right, regardless. They can't never admit bein' wrong."

"What caused the shooting?" Roman asked. "A woman or a poker game?"

"Neither one. Gillum owned a race mare that he bragged could beat any cold-blooded horse in the country. She could scat, all right, and had outrun most of the short horses in Texas. You couldn't blame him for bein' high on her. Well, I had me a little old runty stud that looked like hell wouldn't have him, but he could do a quarter in twenty-two-nine from a standin' start. We matched 'em, lap and tap, and bet everything we had on the race. When my stud ran off and hid on the mare it made Gillum look like a dim-witted dunce. He just couldn't abide bein' so wrong. He called me a crook and grabbed for his gun. I outdrawed him."

"Did you kill him?"

"Deader'n hell."

"The law jump you?"

Brimberry shook his head. "It was purely a case of self-defense. The local sheriff was right there at the time and saw it."

"That doesn't explain why you always carry a gun," Roman said.

"It will, when I tell you that Red Gillum had shirt-tail relations all over Texas. Three days after the shooting his brother Leo came after me with a gun, and ended up the same as Red. Six months later an uncle they called

Big Bill caught up with me over on the Ruidoso and got hisself a slug in the shortribs. Almost a year after that I had to shoot one of Gillum's cousins in Colorado. I don't know how many kinfolk Red had, but it looks like they'll keep comin' at me long as there's a Gillum big enough to trip a trigger. It got downright worrisome, Ben, not knowin' when another would show up."

"So that's why you hired out with Imperial," Roman mused. "You figured the Valley was one place a Gillum wouldn't come hunting for you."

Brimberry nodded. Then he asked, "Who'd you kill?"

"Nobody."

"Then why'd you hire out with Imperial?"

Roman shrugged. "There's no fool like an educated fool," he said.

It was hot in Tucson. The thermometer registered 105 at the Southern Pacific depot. But it was a dry heat that seemed almost pleasant compared to Deseronto's wilting humidity. Ben Roman looked up the railroad's special agent and told him he would pay three dollars a head for laborers, drunk or sober, delivered on the station platform at midnight. Then he said to Brimberry, "You've got until twelve o'clock to sample the wickedness of city life."

"*Bueno,*" Brimberry said, an expectant grin

rutting his russet cheeks. "They say them fancy ladies look real elegant after you've had three drinks of bourbon."

That evening Roman called on Phil Judson, S.P. road-master, who lived in a company house alongside the tracks. "I need laborers," he said. "I've got to have upwards of fifty *muy pronto.*"

Judson shook his head. "They've borrowed every man I could spare off my sections for that flood damage west of Yuma," he said. "A lot of roadbed was under water and they're afraid another flash flood might wash it out. Epes Randolph has ordered seven ballast trains for the job."

"So?"

"A washout there would bust this railroad wide open," Judson explained. "It would put our transcontinental trains out of business for days."

Roman thought about that for a moment before saying, "Then Randolph might be in a good frame of mind to bargain with us right now."

"You mean about buying into Imperial Development?"

Roman nodded.

"Well, I understand that our division engineer told Epes yesterday that nothing less than a concrete gate will keep the Colorado from breaking through at Pilot Knob," Judson said.

"Good! That's the best news I've heard in a long time."

Perhaps, Roman thought, John Chilton was right in predicting that Southern Pacific might come in; that the big thing was to hang on until the necessary funds were available.

Roman said, "You rate pretty high with Randolph, don't you?"

"Just like that," Judson said, holding up two tight fingers. "Epes thinks I'm God's gift to the Maintenance of Way Department."

Mrs. Judson came into the parlor with two bottles of cold beer. She was a tall, rather plain woman in her late forties. Ben Roman rose with the courtesy of a cavalier and asked, "Won't you join us, ma'am?"

"Mercy, no, I never touch beer," Mrs. Jordan said. But she was flattered by the invitation and couldn't help revealing it in the way she smiled.

As she left the room, Roman said, "You're lucky to have so gracious a wife, Phil."

And while Judson was absorbing that pleasant thought, Roman said, "I have reason to believe that Southern Pacific can buy a controlling interest in Imperial Development for around two hundred thousand dollars. That money, of course, would be spent to build a proper gate at Pilot Knob. Why don't you suggest it to Epes Randolph? You could point out that by saving Imperial from bankruptcy, the railroad would be protecting its own interests."

"Why don't you?" Judson asked.

"Wouldn't be the same at all. I'm an Imperial man. He'd be prejudiced against my advice. But coming from you, it would be different, Phil. He'd see the railroad side of it. And if he favors the deal, he's big enough to sell it to the Harrimans."

Judson thought about it. He asked, "Would a concrete gate do the job?"

"Absolutely," Roman said. "There'd never be another breakthrough."

Then, as Judson sat in silent thought, Roman urged, "Think what it might mean to you, Phil. It would be a big deal. One of the biggest in the Southwest. And you'd be the man who got it going."

Judson liked that. He said, "By God, I'll do it. I'll brace Epes first thing in the morning."

Presently, as Roman was leaving, Judson asked, "But how about you, Ben? Won't you be out of a job if S.P. takes over?"

"I've got another proposition in mind."

"Such as what?"

"A wild-horse roundup in the Mogollones."

CHAPTER FOUR

It lacked fifteen minutes of midnight when Ben Roman returned to the Southern Pacific depot, where a crowd awaited the arrival of Westbound Number Six. A gentle breeze, cool and dry, came off the night-cloaked desert, and there was a metallic chattering of telegraph sounders in the lamplit office. Roman walked the length of the platform without seeing Mohee Jim; he looked into the waiting room and then took a turn through a dimly lighted park beyond the depot.

Why wasn't that damned Texan here?

And where was the special agent?

An engine whistled for a road crossing east of town. Number Six, Roman guessed, and pulled out his watch. Five minutes to twelve now, and no sign of Brimberry. No sign of Williams, the special agent, either.

Roman tromped the platform, eyes questing. He observed a saloon across the street and thought: Mohee is probably loading up for the long ride home. Roman hurried over to the saloon.

Brimberry wasn't among the half-dozen customers who stood at the bar. One man slouched over a table at the rear of the dimly lighted room, sleeping off a spree. His face, cradled in the crook of an arm, was hidden, but the steeple-crowned hat on the table was similar to Mohee Jim's Stetson. Roman walked over to the table, grasped a handful of the man's shaggy hair, and lifted his head enough to reveal the face. It wasn't Brimberry. Roman let go the hair, allowing the drunk's face to fall against the table.

When he walked toward the doorway a man asked, "Who you looking for, friend?"

"A tall Texan named Brimberry."

"Don't know him," the man said.

But the bartender announced, "He was in here an hour ago, roaring drunk and looking for a fight with anyone named Gillum."

Roman cursed. He thought: I should've rode herd on the damn fool. Crossing the street now, he heard Number Six pull into the depot. There was no telling where Brimberry was; he might be in any one of a dozen saloons, or spraddled out drunk in some alley, or in some woman's room.

Roman considered going in search of him. But if he did that he would miss the train and thus disrupt his scheduled meeting with his labor-recruiting agents at Gila Bend and Yuma. It looked as if he wasn't going to get a single laborer here, yet Williams had been confident as a man could be. He had said, "Me and the cop on the beat will gather you fifteen or twenty by midnight."

But now, as Roman reached the station platform, there was still no sign of Williams. Or of Mohee Jim.

Westbound passengers were boarding the train. Workmen with grease buckets and long-spouted oilcans swarmed over the engine, inspected car journals and couplings. Roman stood near the smoking car, eagerly scanning faces. It was bad enough to lose Brimberry; but leaving here without at least a dozen laborers meant that his mission had failed. He might pick up seven or eight in Gila Bend, upwards of a dozen in Yuma, but that wouldn't add up to thirty, the minimum requirement.

All the passengers were aboard now. One baggage truck was still loading at the express car. Roman turned to a trainman and asked, "How much time we got left?"

"Five minutes," the man said. "Maybe ten."

Roman walked impatiently along the platform, turned, and was tromping back when he saw Williams come out of the baggage room with a uniformed policeman and several men.

The special agent spotted Roman at once; he called, "We almost didn't make it, mister. Had a heap of trouble with one of these vags."

And now, as the group came closer, Roman recognized Mohee Jim in the group of shabby, sullen men. The crown of Brimberry's hat was mashed flat, one of his eyes was swollen, and blood from a scalp wound trickled down the side of his face.

"What happened to you, Mohee?" Roman asked, delighted to see him.

Brimberry knuckled his purpling right eye. "This cop snuck up on me from behind," he complained. "Took my gun while I was drinkin' at a bar."

"He was threatening to shoot anybody named Gillum," the policeman reported. "Well, my name is Gillum."

Roman chuckled. He said, "I'll pay three dollars for him if you'll return his revolver." And when that had been accomplished, he said to the men, "I'm hiring laborers for Imperial Development. Good wages and good grub. How many of you want to hire out?"

They looked at him, not speaking.

Williams warned, "It's thirty days in jail for those that don't leave town on this train."

And the policeman said grimly, "Hard labor in the chain gang, boys, with grub that ain't fit for hogs."

An old man with wild haunted eyes and a whisker-bristled face said, "I'll go, mister. No more chain gangs for me."

He stepped over beside Roman and was followed by four others.

A trainman called, "All aboard for westbound Number Six! Gila Bend, Yuma,

50

Deseronto, Indio, and Los Angeles!"

"Leave on this train or it's the chain gang," Williams said impatiently. "Work for nothing, or for wages. Make up your minds."

Another man stepped forward, and another; then seven more in a group. That left one man, a huge ape-faced Irishman who muttered, "Ye got no right to crowd me this way, I just finished servin' me time for vag."

"Black Mike Moynihan, pride of the chain gang," the policeman scoffed.

Anger stained Moynihan's round, button-nosed face. "It's a goddamn shanghai deal that's bein' put over!" he objected. "I'll not be bamboozled into your stinkin' scheme!"

Ben Roman waited, thinking now that the big Irishman was worth any three of the others. That brawn would be valuable on the business end of a shovel. He said, "Perhaps Mike is afraid the Red Bull will lick him."

"Who's the Red Bull?" Moynihan demanded. "And what makes ye think I'm scairt of him?"

Roman shrugged. "You aren't the first man who's been afraid of the Red Bull."

"Afraid?" Black Mike asked, his voice high-pitched. "Me, Mike Moynihan, afraid?" He shook his head as if savoring a fantastic and utterly baffling thought; then he bellowed, "Lead me to this Red Bull!"

"Sure," Roman said, not smiling. "I'll lead you to the Red Bull."

Then, allowing his gaze to take them all in, he said, "It's understood that you're staying on this train until it arrives at Deseronto. Any man who attempts to get off will be stopped by Mr. Brimberry, who'll use his gun if necessary."

He turned to Williams and pulled out a roll of bills. "Fifteen at three dollars equals forty-five."

"Correct," William said.

Brimberry led his charges into the smoker. Roman waited until the last recruit was aboard, then stepped up as the train got under way. This, he thought, was a good start. Fifteen men already. There should be enough recruits at Gila Bend and Yuma to more than fill the quota.

A young woman hurried from the waiting room with a cup of coffee in her hand. "Wait!" she cried. "Wait for me!"

The train was picking up speed as Roman leaned out and grasped her outstretched hand. He hauled her up, got an arm around her. Then, as wind plucked the little black pancake hat from her head, she made a grab for it — with the hand that held the cup of coffee. The hot liquid splashed into Ben Roman's face. He cursed and pulled her into the vestibule and blinked coffee out of his eyes.

"Oh, I'm sorry!" the blonde young woman gasped.

"You should be," Roman muttered, wiping his face on a shirt sleeve. "You sure as hell should be."

Whereupon he turned his back to her and went into the smoking car.

CHAPTER FIVE

Brimberry sat facing the seats occupied by the fifteen recruits. He gawked at Ben Roman and demanded, "What in hell happened to you, Ben?"

"Fool woman dumped a cup of coffee in my face," Roman said.

Black Mike Moynihan loosed a hoot of jeering laughter. He pointed a huge hair-tufted finger at Roman's coffee-sogged shirt and shouted, "She must've mistook ye for a slop bucket!"

Roman ignored him, whereupon Moynihan proclaimed, "Look at him, boys — a slop bucket with ears!"

"Shut up, you north-of-Ireland ape," Roman muttered.

Moynihan reared up from his seat and roared, "I'll take no goddamn insults from ye!"

"Sit down," Roman ordered, wanting no trouble on the train.

But Black Mike Moynihan was in a fighting mood, and he dearly loved an audience. " 'Tis in me mind to teach ye some respect for the Irish," he announced. "Put up yer hands and fight!"

Roman shook his head. "Not on this train."

Moynihan's hooting laughter rose above the clickety-clack of wheels crossing rail joints. He looked at his grinning companions; he pinched his button nose between thumb and forefinger and asked loudly, "De ye smell a bad odor, boys — like somethin' was rotten spoilt?"

Mohee Jim got out of his seat. He drew his gun and waggled it at Moynihan, commanding, "Sit down, you flannel-mouthed Mick!"

"Ah, another smart one," Moynihan jeered, transferring his attention to Brimberry. "I'll snatch that pistol away and ram it down yer throat."

"You won't get that close to me," Brimberry said, thumbing back the hammer of his revolver.

Roman motioned Brimberry back. But the Texan came along the aisle and muttered, "I'll fix the big baboon. I'll fix him good."

Roman lunged past Moynihan, blocking off Brimberry. Then he turned and said, "Sit down, Mike, before you get hurt."

"Make me," Moynihan said, eagerness glinting his round black eyes. "Make me sit down."

Roman shrugged. He glanced past Moynihan and said, "All right, brakeman. Hit him with your club."

Black Mike whirled, throwing up an arm to ward off an expected blow. He was like that, half turned, when Roman pitched forward and hit him on the jaw.

The impact of knuckles against flesh made a meaty smack that was repeated as Roman struck again, targeting Moynihan's nose. As the Irishman's arms came up to guard his face, Roman slugged him in the belly.

"Pour it on him!" Mohee Jim yelled.

Black Mike retreated, evading Roman's fists. He shook his head as if dazed, and twin trickles of blood appeared below his flattened nostrils. But Roman thought: I haven't really hurt him, and marveled at that knowledge.

Rage flowed out of Black Mike in a bellowing roar. "Ye sneakin' smart-alecky son-of-a-bitch!" he shouted.

Then he charged forward with huge fists cocked like clubs.

They stood toe to toe for a moment, slugging and being slugged, while the car's passengers shouted gleeful appreciation and a trainman, entering from the rear vestibule, demanded, "What's going on in here?"

Roman took a glancing blow that raked a ribbon of skin from his right cheek; he countered with a smash that caught Moynihan just below his high-arched ribs, driving the wind out of him. When Moynihan's guard came down Roman hit him in the face with successive rights and lefts.

"You've got him!" Mohee Jim shouted.

Moynihan was wholly on the defensive

now, staggering backward like a drunken man. As Roman drove him along the aisle, he tripped over the out-thrust boot of a conniving spectator. "Now ye get yer needin's, by God!" he roared.

Moynihan hit Roman with a chopping right that knocked him against a seat. Roman clawed for the big man's legs, and missed them, and fell sideways as the train lurched into a sharp curve. Thrown off balance, Moynihan grasped a seat to steady himself. In this momentary cessation of hostilities, Roman regained his feet.

The big Irishman was on him instantly. Roman ducked, driving a shoulder against Moynihan's flogging right arm. Another lurch of the train threw them across the aisle together and they remained there, pounding each other with short fast blows, panting and grunting and using their knees. Roman was remotely aware of the conductor coming into the car and shouting, "Stop that! Stop it, I say!"

Roman slugged Moynihan in the belly with a blow that made Black Mike squall a curse; he ducked a sledging right and hit the big man on the jaw just as the train tilted sharply into another curve. Moynihan reached out and tried to save himself and couldn't. He fell headlong, striking his temple on the metal stanchion of a seat, and went limp.

Roman wiped his bloody knuckles on his pants. He peered down at Moynihan and said, "Might be hurt," and watched as the brakeman turned Black Mike over on his back.

There was a red welt across Moynihan's forehead. His eyes were open and blankly staring; his slack-jawed face was smeared with blood.

"Hit his head hard enough to bust it," the brakeman said.

Roman nodded. As the conductor came for his look at the unconscious Irishman, he asked, "Have you a doctor on the train?"

"How would I know?" the conductor said. He picked up Moynihan's limp left arm and felt for a pulse; then he said to the brakeman, "Go see if there's a doctor aboard, and hurry!"

It seemed a long time before the brakeman came back and said, "Here's a doctor."

Ben Roman was down on his knees, supporting Moynihan's head against the car's continuous jolting. He eased around, making room in the narrow aisle. He saw a woman's trim ankles and a skirt, and, glancing quickly up, saw an oval face framed by high-coiled blonde hair. The face of the young woman who'd spilled coffee on him.

"You?" he said. "Where's the doctor?"

She knelt beside him and felt of Moynihan's wrist with slender fingers and said, "I'm the doctor."

It didn't make sense to Ben Roman. A woman doctor? He had never heard of such a thing.

When she leaned forward to examine the welt on Moynihan's head, Roman became aware of a subtle feminine fragrance that seemed out of place in this foul-odored car.

"Is he hurt, ma'am?" the conductor inquired.

"I believe it's just a slight concussion," she reported, lifting Moynihan's eyelids in turn and examining their lining. "His pulse is very strong, and he's breathing normally now."

She reached into the medicine kit beside her, took out a small green bottle, and, removing its stopper, held the bottle to Black Mike's bloody nostrils.

Roman smelled the stinging odor of ammonia. He thought, Moynihan needs something stronger than that. But now the big man moved and drew a deep breath.

The lady doctor stood up. She said, "He'll come out of it now." Glancing at Roman's blood-smeared knuckles, she asked, "Are you the one who knocked him down?"

Roman nodded. "Just a little friendly argument."

"Friendly?" she asked, giving the word a derisive emphasis.

Moynihan hunched up on his elbows. He shook his head and peered about him in dazed wonderment and shook his head again. "What the hell?" he mumbled.

Then, as his eyes came into focus, he peered up at Ben Roman and blurted, "Why, ye smart-alecky spalpeen!"

Roman stepped back as Moynihan got up. He said, "Take it easy, Mike."

And the conductor warned, "No more rough stuff on this train."

But Black Mike ignored them. He shouted, "I'll teach ye some proper respect for the Irish!" and lunged forward.

Roman side-stepped, evading a wild swing. He grasped the front of Moynihan's shirt and yanked him into a pivoting turn. Taking deliberate aim, Roman clouted him hard below the left ear and heard the lady doctor exclaim, "You brute! You awful brute!"

Moynihan teetered drunkenly. A wild confusion came into his glazing eyes, and his shoulders sagged. But he continued to swing his right arm.

"Quit, you fool," Roman muttered, still clutching Black Mike's shirt and taking his ineffectual blows on shoulder and ribs.

Moynihan was blind now, out on his feet. But the instinct to attack was an unreasoning rage in him. His right fist was still weakly swinging when Roman measured him again, and again slugged him below the ear. Then, as Moynihan went limp, Roman pushed him to the end of a seat and let him collapse into it.

"Mule-stubborn," a man said.

"And mule-strong," Roman muttered. Turning to the lady doctor, he asked, "How much do I owe you, ma'am?"

She eyed him with unconcealed contempt. She said, "Two dollars is the usual fee."

"Anything extra for train calls?"

She shook her head.

"I'll need your name for my expense account," Roman said.

"Lee Farnum," she said, adding quickly, "Dr. Lee Farnum."

"A pleasure to meet you," Roman said, not smiling, and paid her the two dollars.

"Thank you, Mr. —"

"Roman." He looked her in the eye. "Brute Roman."

There was no break in the professional way she looked at him, and her voice was wholly impersonal when she said, "I owe you something for assisting me onto the train."

She reached over and tucked the two bills into his shirt pocket. Then she picked up her medical kit and walked primly toward the rear vestibule.

"A lady doctor," Mohee Jim mused in a disbelieving voice.

Even the conductor seemed unwilling to accept the fact. "Maybe she's just a nurse, running a bluff on us," he suggested. Glancing at Moynihan, who was now sleeping soundly, the conductor asked, "Has he got a ticket?"

61

"I'm paying his fare to Deseronto," Roman said, "and sixteen others."

Afterward Roman borrowed some salt from a porter and soaked the puffed knuckles of his right hand for upwards of an hour. There was a kindred soreness along his rib section, where Moynihan's big fists had pounded him. He thought: I'll be lame as a foundered horse tomorrow.

Black Mike would also be lame. That Mick, Roman reflected, was a real battler. Game as a wild stallion. One knockout punch hadn't been enough to stop him. It had taken two.

Roman grinned, thinking how those final punches had caused the lady doctor to call him a brute. Lee Farnum, he supposed, was fresh out of some Eastern medical school. She probably wasn't more than twenty-three or -four years old, and thought she knew it all.

When the train rolled into Gila Bend, a special agent was waiting on the platform with seven shabby recruits, two of them so drunk they had to be helped aboard. "A sorry-looking bunch of bums," Roman said, paying off. "Not a real worker in the lot."

But he was well pleased. Twenty-two laborers already. He smiled, thinking how happy John Chilton would be. It wouldn't occur to John that these men had been shanghaied. The softhearted general manager would muck out the canal with his bare hands before he'd use such a method of acquiring help. But John wouldn't ask questions.

Roman eased back in his seat, fully relaxed. The car's warm, smoke-fouled air made him drowsy. He looked over at Moynihan, saw that the Irishman was still sleeping, and closed his eyes. This trip was going to be a success. In addition to furnishing a much-needed construction crew, it would force Angus MacIvor to remain on the job for six months. By that time Epes Randolph might decide to throw Southern Pacific's huge resources into an all-out effort against the Red Bull.

That was the one chance for the project's survival. The only chance.

And John Chilton knew it; he knew that the river couldn't be controlled with make-shifts. Thinking about Chilton now, Roman wondered how any man could remain faithful to a dream so long, and at such cost.

Afterward, as the train rushed on through the night, Roman remembered Lee Farnum's lilac perfume, and wondered if she would be on the train at breakfasttime.

She was.

She sat alone at a table in the diner, garbed in a fashionable powder-gray dress with a high, lace-trimmed collar. She looked fresh and dainty as a queen. Roman thumbed the bristle of whiskers on his bruised cheek and supposed he looked like a tramp, but he sat down at her table and said, "Good morning, Doc."

She lowered her coffee cup. She said, "Good morning, Mr. —" and seemed unable to recall his name.

"Roman," he said. "Brute Roman. Remember?"

Lee Farnum smiled and went on with her breakfast, not speaking again until Roman had been served. Then she asked, "How is your Irish friend?"

"A trifle grumpy, but peaceable," Roman reported, aware of her perfume now and liking it.

Presently he asked, "Have you been a doctor long, ma'am?"

That seemed to embarrass her. "Not very long," she admitted. Then, as if confessing a shameful thing, she said, "Your friend was my first patient."

Roman chuckled. "Moynihan will feel highly honored. He's probably the only man west of the Pecos to be a lady doctor's first patient."

"West of the Pecos," she mused, liking the phrase. She looked out at the desert's vast sunlit emptiness for a moment before saying, "The country is so big it makes one feel small and unimportant."

It occurred to Roman that he'd heard John

Chilton express the same sentiment in the same tone of voice.

"It makes you feel like doing something big — something really important," she went on. "No wonder they call it the land of opportunity."

Roman laughed. "How far east you come from, Doc?"

"Buffalo, New York."

"Well, I know a man who came from Syracuse, and he felt the same way. He wanted to do something big and important."

"Did he?"

Roman shrugged. "He's been taking a beating for years, trying to. It's made an old man out of him."

"Not you?"

"Hell, no. I can take the desert or leave it alone. Being in a big country doesn't make me ambitious. Works the other way. Makes me feel sort of contented. But not my friend from Syracuse. He's got to change it. Improve it for other folks. No matter what it costs him, or how long it takes, he's got to keep trying, regardless."

Lee Farnum nodded. "I can understand that. It's the trying that makes life worth living."

"So?"

"Well, the least anyone can do is try."

Roman shook his head. "What's so worth while about butting your head against a stone

65

wall? A thumb-sucking dunce should know better than that."

A rebellious brightness came into Lee Farnum's eyes and she said, "That's what they told me when I decided to be a doctor. They did everything to discourage me. My family, my friends. Even the professors at school. They all tried to stop me. They said it was a man's profession."

"Well, isn't it?"

She resented that, and showed it in the way she got up from the table. "You men are all alike," she accused. "You think a woman should aspire to be nothing more than a married drudge!"

She turned to the steward, paid her bill, and went on back to her Pullman.

Lady doctor, Roman thought disgustedly. Why weren't women satisfied to be women, the way God made them? What was the world coming to, with women wanting to be doctors, and suffragettes, and the Lord knew what else?

Why couldn't they be like Slim Lacey — just women? He grinned, thinking of the turquoise bracelet he'd bought in Tucson for Slim. There, by God, was a female woman. If a man ever decided to get married, she'd make him a grand wife. But that's the only way he'd ever get her — with a wedding ring.

The train had stopped briefly at a way station. Now, as it went on, a brakeman came

66

into the dining car and announced, "Telegram for Ben Roman!"

The message, from John Chilton, was brief:

HAVE BEEN CALLED TO LOS ANGELES FOR CONSULTATION. YOU TAKE CHARGE AS GENERAL MANAGER.

The twenty-two labor recruits were eating box lunches in the smoker as the train rolled into the station at Yuma. When it pulled out, Ben Roman ordered twelve more lunches.

"Thirty-four men!" Mohee Jim grinned. "You've done won your bet with MacIvor."

Roman nodded. But there was no enthusiasm in him, no exuberance. He peered at the Colorado's brown slow-flowing water as the train inched across the bridge at reduced speed. The recent flash flood had gouged deep caverns in the west bank; it had cut new channels and left stagnant pools of water on the brush-tangled flats.

Black Mike Moynihan came over to Roman's seat. He said, "They tell me the Red Bull is a river."

"Yes," Roman said. "A ringtailed heller of a river."

An expression of deep disappointment rutted Moynihan's fist-scarred face. "Ye fooled me with that talk about the Red Bull," he accused.

Roman nodded. "Maybe I fooled myself, too."

When Black Mike went back to his seat, Roman showed Mohee Jim the telegram from John Chilton. "That is Clark Hazelhurst's doings," he muttered.

"You reckon they'll fire Chilton?" Brimberry asked.

"They might. And if they do, I'll give Hazelhurst the beating of his life."

"Then quit the project?"

Roman nodded.

Mohee Jim liked that. He said smilingly, "I got a hunch we'll make that wild-horse gather in the Mogollones."

CHAPTER SIX

Angus MacIvor stood in the doorway of Lacey's Restaurant and stared at the group of men being herded toward Imperial's office building by Mohee Jim Brimberry. "It's fantastic!" MacIvor exclaimed.

Slim Lacey joined him in the doorway. She saw Ben Roman bring up the rear of the procession with a big man whose eyes were swollen to discolored slits. There was a scar on Ben's cheek and he looked tired. When he saw them standing there he waved and called, "Count 'em, Angus."

He angled across the street and handed Slim a small package. "Present from a man in Tucson," he announced.

"Who?" Slim asked.

"Didn't give his name," Roman said. Quartering back across Main Street, he added, "Just told me it was for the prettiest girl in Deseronto."

MacIvor was making a count of the laborers: "Twenty-seven, twenty-eight, twenty-nine . . ." he tallied aloud.

Frank Monroe came over from his newspaper office. "Looks as if Roman has acquired a new construction crew," he said thoughtfully. "Wonder where he got all those men."

"That's what I'd like to know," MacIvor muttered. "Where could he get thirty-four men to come here at this time of year?"

"Perhaps he offered them a bonus," Slim suggested.

As MacIvor turned to follow the procession, Monroe said, "By the looks of them, I'd be more inclined to guess they were forced to come."

"Ben wouldn't do a thing like that," Slim objected.

Monroe gave her a lingering appraisal. He had been in Deseronto less than four months, a flat-chested, scholarly young man who seemed content to live frugally while composing controversial editorials for his Weekly Clarion. But it was no secret that he had a case on Slim Lacey; he revealed it each time he looked at her. Now he said in a mildly censuring way, "I thought you considered Ben Roman a thick-skinned Texas tough. I thought we agreed that he cared nothing for the settlers, or for the workers he drove so mercilessly, or anyone else."

Slim nodded. "That's what I thought, Frank. But now I'm not so sure."

"Why?"

"Well, I think he's been very loyal to John Chilton, for one thing."

Afterward, as Monroe ate his noon meal at

the counter, he said, "Don't be fooled by a man like Roman. His kind take what they want and give nothing in return."

Slim was considering that when Mohee Jim Brimberry came into the restaurant. "What a night!" He climbed onto a stool and fanned himself with his hat. "Them bums tried to escape every time the train stopped. They sure kept me busy."

"Ah, so Roman did get them by force," Monroe said with a sly glance at Slim.

"Sure. Ben had to beat up one big Mick. Had to knock him cold as a cucumber."

Monroe took a notebook from his hip pocket. He said, "Sounds like an interesting story, Mohee. Where did those men come from?"

"Perhaps Ben wouldn't want it told," Slim suggested.

But Mohee Jim said confidently, "Ben don't give a damn for nothin' or nobody. You should of saw him stand up to Black Mike Moynihan. That Irishman outweighs Ben by better'n forty pounds, I reckon. He used to be steel gang boss on the Union Pacific. He's got fists on him big as slop buckets. But Ben knocked him out, and it took a medico to revive him."

"Did Moynihan object to being brought here?" Monroe inquired.

"Object? I'll say he objected. When he came to he started fighting some more, and

Ben had to bust him down again." Mohee chuckled, recalling how it was. He said, "That was the damnedest train fight you ever saw. Lasted for upwards of forty miles."

Monroe made penciled notes as Brimberry talked. When it was over he said, "Thanks for a good story, Mohee," and departed.

Slim refilled Brimberry's coffee cup. She said, "Ben may not like all that being in the newspaper."

"What difference would it make?" Mohee Jim asked. "We got them men here, didn't we? And now the canal can be mucked out."

Slim thought about that for a moment before saying, "Yes, I suppose that's the important thing. I guess Ben thinks nothing else matters, just so he can finish the job."

"Naw, it ain't that at all. He wanted to win a bet with Angus MacIvor. Ben is quittin' this outfit. Me and him have other plans."

"A wild-horse roundup?" Slim asked.

Mohee Jim nodded. "We'll make us a mint of money," he predicted.

Other customers came in: Lew Gallatin, who ran the tent saloon; Dr. Shumway, who was never quite drunk and never quite sober; and Swede Erickson, the blacksmith. They were, Slim thought, as unlike as three men could be. Gallatin dressed like a sport and talked like a sport; believing himself attractive to women, he assumed an intimacy that didn't exist, asking, "Why so sad, Slim honey?"

Doc Shumway, who was in his late thirties and looked ten years older, ignored women, being securely wedded to alcohol. Swede Erickson, huge and homely and bashful, looked upon all women in the worshipful way of a lonely bachelor wanting a wife.

Serving them, and taking pains to keep beyond reach of Lew Gallatin's restless fingers, Slim thought about Ben Roman, who was neither sporty nor bashful nor unaware of women. He was somewhat like her father — a born drifter who'd not be content to stay long in one place. Nor, she supposed, with one woman.

Presently, when her customers had eaten and departed, Slim opened the small package Ben had given her. The bracelet was beautiful, its green-blue stones perfectly matched for size and color. She clasped it on her wrist and admired it, and marveled that Ben Roman should have given her so fine a gift.

The same Ben Roman who was quitting Imperial Development when the project needed him most.

A born drifter.

"Darn him," Slim whispered. "Darn him, anyway!"

CHAPTER SEVEN

Angus MacIvor looked at the thirty-four men who had formed a line along the front of Imperial's general office. Except for one man, who'd evidently lost his hat and was now wearing a soiled shirt over his head like a shawl, they appeared to be in normal possession of their wits. Not overly bright, perhaps, but not drooling idiots. Yet they had come here in August. . . .

"It's fantastic," MacIvor muttered.

Black Mike Moynihan, at the head of the line, mopped his battered face with a sweat-soaked bandanna. "What a stinkin' furnace of a place!" he complained. " 'Tis not fit for man or beast."

"Then why did you come here?" MacIvor asked.

Moynihan scowled at him. "Who the hell might you be?"

"My name is MacIvor, and I'm chief engineer of this project, God help me."

One of the drunks who'd been carried on at Yuma stood in shoulder-slumped dejection with tears dribbling down his whisker-stubbled cheeks. "An oven, if ever I saw one," he sobbed. "That's what it is. An oven."

Now, as Ben Roman stepped out of the office followed by George Frayne, Moynihan demanded, "When do we eat?"

"Soon as you get on the payroll and choose a cook," Roman said. "I'm making you foreman of this gang."

Moynihan squinted at him through swollen eyelids. "Ye mean that I'm to be the boss?"

Roman nodded. "You'll run this gang your own way, just so the work gets done."

"Well, now," Moynihan mused. "That's more like it. And where do I find this Red Bull river ye want put in its place?"

"At Pilot Knob. Mohee Jim will furnish you wagons for the trip. Meet George Frayne, our chief clerk, who'll sign you boys on."

Frayne winced as Moynihan grasped his hand. Retrieving his slender fingers, Frayne peered at them as if expecting to see blood.

"Put Mike on the payroll as foreman, and be sure he gets what he needs from the commissary," Roman directed.

"But Tony Caruso is gang foreman at Pilot Knob," Frayne objected.

"There'll be two gangs and two foremen," Roman explained. "Just do as I say, George."

"Caruso — an Eyetalian?" Moynihan asked.

When Roman nodded, Black Mike asked disgustedly, "Now, why would ye have an Eyetalian foreman?"

"Tony has a small gang," Roman said. Then he added with sly emphasis, "But he knows how to get a day's work out of a man."

"Ah, he does, does he? Well, I'll make him look like a pimply-faced dude fresh out of Kansas City."

When the necessary arrangements had been made for the gang's transportation by wagon to Pilot Knob, Roman went into John Chilton's office. According to Frayne, there was an important letter for him on Chilton's desk. Roman picked up the sealed envelope, eased into a chair, opened the envelope, and read the penciled message:

Dear Ben:
They have called me into headquarters for what may be dismissal. If that proves to be the case, I shall do everything in my power to have you appointed general manager. It is not important who completes the project, just so it is completed. After your departure for Tucson I made arrangements with the U.S. Weather Bureau to telegraph immediate reports of extensive rainfall anywhere in the Colorado watershed. With that information we should be able to anticipate high water before it reaches Yuma and thus be prepared for it.

Perhaps my dismissal, if it should come, will prove a Godsend, as I fear that my heart, which has bothered me much of late, is in bad shape. In any event, Ben, remember what your father said in Texas and be guided by it. The Imperial Valley project is more important than any of the people connected with it.

Please keep that uppermost in mind during the days to come, and what ever they may bring.

Your friend,
JOHN

Ben Roman swore softly. He got up and was pouring himself a drink of water from the olla when George Frayne opened the inner door. "There's a lady to see you," the chief clerk announced.

"A lady, to see me?"

"Well, she asked for the general manager."

"Tell her he's out of town."

"But Mr. Chilton said you were —"

"Tell her," Roman commanded, "that he's out of town!"

"She's very eager to —"

Roman cursed. He flung the tin cup at Frayne and yelled, "Git!"

The cup struck Frayne's shoulder. But most of its contents splashed into the face of a young woman who had come to the doorway behind him.

Roman stared at her in squint-eyed wonderment. He said, "The lady doctor," and watched as she dabbed at her face with a handkerchief.

Lee Farnum exclaimed, "You?" And when he nodded she asked, "Are you the general manager?"

"For the time being. Won't you come in?"

She asked, "Is it safe?"

Roman grinned. He said, "I'm sorry about the water," and offered her a chair.

"You should be," she said emphatically, making futile dabs at the water stains on her blouse. "You sure as hell should be!"

Then, as two slim fingers darted to her lips in a girlish gesture of embarrassment, Roman loosed a great whoop of laughter. "Such language from a lady doctor!"

Glancing at George Frayne, who stood staring in the doorway, Roman said, "She's from Buffalo. Buffalo, New York," and let laughter claim him.

"What's so comical about that?" Lee Farnum demanded.

And then she, too, was laughing.

George Frayne, completely baffled, backed out of the office and closed the door.

"He thinks we're loco," Roman chuckled.

Lee Farnum nodded and, glancing at her wet blouse, said, "Perhaps we are." Then she asked, "Where is my office?"

"Your office?"

She nodded. "I'm replacing a Dr. Shumway who I understand is about to retire."

It took a moment for Ben Roman to comprehend the significance of her words. When full understanding came he thought: Those damn fools in Los Angeles!

He asked, "Do they know you're a woman?"

"Well, my application didn't say so, specifically. It was signed Lee Farnum, M.D., which is how any physician would sign an application."

"And you let them think you were a man," Roman accused.

She shrugged. "What difference does it make?"

"Plenty," Roman said.

He looked at the black, veil-trimmed little hat perched atop her high-piled hair; the frilly blue blouse and stylish skirt. He thought of what the desert would do to her. . . .

"This is no job for a lady doctor," he said flatly.

"What possible difference can my sex make?" she demanded. "A doctor is a doctor. Pain has no sex, nor does the cure of it."

Roman rejected that philosophy with a shrug; he said, "Your patients won't all be where you can walk to them. And there'd be times when you couldn't use a buggy. Were you ever on a horse?"

When she shook her head, Roman asked, "Suppose a man gets hurt back in the brush

79

where there's no road?"

"I can learn to ride horseback," Lee Farnum said, very confident about this. "It's not an exact science requiring months of study."

Roman gave his attention to shaping a cigarette. Here, he decided, was a woman who thought she was equal to a man; or superior, most likely. A know-it-all, fresh out of medical school, and expecting to get by on her good looks. He said, "There's more to it than learning to stay on a horse. There's heat, and sandstorms, and men all messed up in construction accidents. It's just no job for a woman."

Lee Farnum peered at him in the patient way of a schoolteacher contemplating a very stubborn and very stupid pupil. "I am normally resourceful and adequately equipped with medical knowledge," she said. "Those are the basic requirements."

"But it's no job for a lady doctor," Roman insisted.

"What utter nonsense!" Then, as if shrugging off something that really didn't matter, she got up from the chair and asked, "Where is my office?"

Roman remained seated. "Used to having your own way, aren't you? Well, you've got no office here while I'm in charge."

"But I've been hired by the Los Angeles headquarters," she said.

Roman inhaled tobacco smoke and allowed it to filter leisurely from his nostrils before saying, "Then go to work there."

He watched anger warm her eyes and stain her cheeks. It was an odd thing. She had seemed cold and aloof a moment ago; now she was all fire and passion. Even her lips seemed redder and fuller as she exclaimed, "You hidebound mule!"

Roman got up and flipped his cigarette through the doorway and said, "You're not being forced to associate with a mule."

When she stood there, making no move to depart, he said, "You'd better go."

"I never heard of such ill manners," Lee Farnum protested.

Roman laughed at her.

"Why, you — you idiot!" she cried.

And then she slapped him.

Roman reached out and grasped her by both arms with anger-prodded violence. Her hair came down in disorder and her hat fell to the floor. Struggling to pull free, she was like a panting dancer. There was nothing haughty about her now.

"Pretty," Roman said. "Pretty enough to kiss."

"Take your filthy hands off me!" she cried.

Instead, Roman pulled her close, and, missing her mouth, drew his lips across her cheek.

"Don't you dare!"

Roman used his shoulder to force her face around. He inhaled deeply, as if savoring a delectable fragrance, and said smilingly, "Always did admire lilac perfume."

Then he found her lips.

Lee Farnum ceased struggling while he kissed her. Accepting the kiss without response, she remained passive, as if waiting for him to finish, and when he released her she asked calmly, "Are you through?"

It was like another slap in the face to Ben Roman. He watched as she rearranged her tumbled hair. When he picked up the hat and handed it to her she asked, "Do you always kiss women employees?"

"Only the ones that slap me," Roman said.

She walked over to the doorway and turned and said, "I'm going to remain in Deseronto and I'm going to show you what a woman doctor can do."

Roman was watching her go along the plank walk toward the Empire Hotel when George Frayne stepped up behind him and announced, "Here's a weather report that says it's raining hard in the Grand Tetons and the Medicine Bow range."

Roman read the report, then walked over to scan the wall map behind Chilton's desk.

"That would be the Green River," Frayne said, eager to demonstrate his knowledge of the Colorado watershed. "It's the largest tributary, rising in the Wind River Mountains of

Wyoming and receiving the runoff from the Grand Tetons. Down below there, in Colorado, it's joined by the Little Snake, which drains the Medicine Bow."

Roman peered at the map, estimating the miles. "A long way off," he mused. "Shouldn't bother us much down here, unless there's other rains."

Motioning to Chilton's desk, he said, "Sit down there and take a letter to Florsheim."

And when Frayne was ready, Roman dictated: "Mr. Ronald Florsheim, President, Imperial Development Company, Los Angeles, California. Dear Mr. Florsheim: This is to inform you that dismissal of John Chilton as general manager here will result in my immediate resignation."

"You mean you'd quit, even if they made you general manager?" Frayne demanded.

Roman nodded. "Add to that line — my immediate resignation and that of our chief engineer, Angus MacIvor. I have just recruited a force of thirty-four laborers, which will give the project a good chance for surviving the present emergency if these arrangements are not disrupted by a change in management here. However, I shall not put these men to work until advised what your decision is regarding John Chilton."

Frayne stared at him. He said, "Some men work all their lives for a chance to be general manager."

"Perhaps they'll give you the job," Roman said.

"Oh, no," Frayne said, visibly perturbed by the mere mention of it. "There'd be too much responsibility — too many decisions for me to make."

Roman grinned at him. He said, "You're smarter than you look, George."

Frayne glanced at his notes. "Is that all?"

Roman nodded.

"How about the lady doctor? Shouldn't you say something about her?"

Roman shook his head. "John can take care of that when he returns."

"But suppose he doesn't?"

Roman made a chopping motion with his right hand. "Don't ask damn-fool questions!"

The day operator from the Southern Pacific depot came into the office and announced, "An important telegram for you, Mr. Roman."

"More rain?" Roman asked, and took the telegram.

It said:

JOHN CHILTON DIED THIS MORNING OF HEART ATTACK. IT WAS HIS DYING WISH THAT YOU REPLACE HIM AS GENERAL MANAGER IN CHARGE FIELD OPERATIONS. BOARD OF DIRECTORS HAS ACCORDINGLY APPOINTED YOU TO THAT POSITION.
RONALD FLORSHEIM

Ben Roman cursed softly. He said, "Poor John." Then he handed the telegram to George Frayne and said, "You can tear up my letter."

Roman went out into the sun-hammered street and walked toward Gallatin's saloon, not realizing that he had forgotten to put on his hat.

The news of John Chilton's death spread rapidly through Deseronto. Men shook their heads and discussed his passing with dismay. "Another catastrophe," they said. "The Valley is doomed."

By sundown the news had spread to settlers' homes far out on the flats — to grim-faced men with callused hands, and to the weary women who shared their shacks. It turned them morose, and more apprehensive than the flood damage had made them. For even though John Chilton had thus far failed to control the Colorado, he had assumed the stature of a miracle-maker to men who had seen desert dust transformed into gardens of summer squash, pumpkins, cucumbers, cantaloupes, and lima beans; who had harvested vast fields of barley and sorghum; who had seen milo grow tall as a cow. Observing Chilton's rejection of surrender each time the control gates failed, these men had taken another grip on the long handle of his hope.

To the settlers John Chilton had been more

than general manager of Imperial Development. He *was* Imperial Development.

These men peered out across flood-ravaged fields and asked themselves: What will we do now?

CHAPTER EIGHT

Ben Roman sat alone at a table in Gallatin's tent saloon and cursed the green-bellied flies that pestered him. Heat came through the canvas roof; it radiated from the clapboard siding and from the rammed-earth floor. Roman wiped his sweaty face on a shirt sleeve and poured himself a drink, observing that the bottle was more than half full. He had intended to get drunk. Roaring, forgetting drunk. But whisky didn't melt the knot of humility inside him, or banish the realization that John Chilton, in dying, had fashioned a trap for him.

What, Roman wondered, made a man do what John had done?

There had been no greed in Chilton; no hope of recouping a lost fortune. Nor had there been any grasping for glory.

Why, then, had John spent his final spark of energy arranging for a successor, voicing one last wish that must be granted?

Again, as he so often had, Roman marveled at the man's unwavering faith, and tried to understand it, and could not. Nor could he understand the deep sense of loss Chilton's death had brought him. There'd been no close bond of friendship between them, no mutual attraction of kindred souls; just a fragile strand of allegiance sprouted from the seed of long association.

Roman watched Lew Gallatin light the saloon's three-bracket lamps. Must be getting late; way past suppertime, he supposed. Gallatin asked, "How you like that Colonel's Monogram bourbon, Ben?"

"It's all right," Roman said.

"Supposed to be high-class merchandise," Gallatin bragged, and went behind the bar.

High-class, hell, Roman thought. More likely it was some diluted bargain bought from a jackleg peddler. Lew Gallatin was in business to make an easy dollar. Everything about this makeshift saloon showed it. And there was the shack out back with a board fence around it, where French Nellie entertained amorous visitors. She belonged to Lew, the same as this tent; a money-making property.

Observing how hale and hearty Lew Gallatin appeared, Roman thought: He's alive and John is dead. Where's the justice in that?

Why was the good man taken and the spoiler spared?

He had wondered about that when his father died; he had looked at boozy old bums in town and resented their survival. A teenaged boy then, he'd supposed there was some right and reasonable answer. But he had not

88

found it, nor could he find it now.

Presently, as Doc Shumway came toward him with a filled shot glass in hand, Roman thought: The damn counterfeit wants company.

Doc halted, and indecision marked his watery eyes. He stood for a moment, plainly wanting an invitation; when it didn't come he asked, "Mind if I join you?"

Roman shrugged, and Shumway eased into a chair, saying, "It's a sad thing about John Chilton." He sampled his drink, grimacing as he swallowed. "John had great vision and great courage. His death is a loss to us all."

Roman nodded.

"Few men could have weathered the storms of adversity as John weathered them," Shumway said. "Losing a beautiful wife would have ruined most men." His spongy, perspiring face was wholly grave as he added bitterly, "It ruined me."

The thought came to Ben Roman that he had despised this drunkard doctor without ever wondering what had made him turn to whisky. Now he prompted, "So it was a woman."

Shumway nodded. "The most beautiful woman who ever lived. My wife, Rosalea."

"Did she run off with another man?" Roman asked.

Shumway gulped down the remainder of his drink and grimaced again. "She died," he said, and toyed with the empty glass, rolling it back and forth between his deft surgeon's fingers. "Seven years ago come September."

Observing the way he glanced at the bottle, Roman understood that Doc was itching for another drink. The bottle was uncorked, its aromatic odor quite strong. Roman said, "Have one on me," and pushed the bottle across the table.

"Well, thanks," Shumway said. He licked his lips. He nudged his dust-speckled derby farther back on his head. Then he took out his watch and looked at it and said, "Not for another fifty minutes."

"You're spacing your drinks?"

Shumway nodded. "I limit myself to one an hour," he explained. A self-mocking smile creased his cheeks as he added, "A matter of conscience, in case someone needs me. By such spacing I'm never quite drunk."

Never quite sober, either, Roman thought. But he had a better feeling toward Doc now. Presently he asked, "Was your wife young when she died?"

"In the first bloom of womanhood. That perfect blend of girl and woman that some brides bring to their husbands. She had lovely eyes. Blue-gray, like wood smoke on a clear morning. And dark chestnut hair that had a soft sheen to it. I used to watch her arrange it, marveling at the deft sure movement of her fingers. There is something wholly feminine about the ritual."

Doc was silent for a long moment, as if entranced by a picture of his wife sitting before her mirror. Then he said, "I suppose all brides are beautiful to their husbands. The reflected images of each man's dream of what a woman's face and body should be. But her real beauty was an inner thing. A graciousness, and a love of life. She was easy to smile, my Rosalea. We were very happy together." Shumway chuckled, remembering how it had been. "It seems a trifle odd now, but she called me the most manly of men."

There was an expression on Doc's face that Roman had not seen before: a look of pride and tranquillity that lingered for a moment and was gone.

"How did she die?"

"Ruptured appendix. I did all that any surgeon could have done. But it wasn't enough. The day after Rosalea's funeral I gave up my practice, went to another city, and then another." Doc shrugged. "The traveling made no difference. Nothing did. Not even whisky. I couldn't forget that Rosalea was sure I would save her — and how utterly I failed."

Roman nodded sympathetically. "Now you're trapped. And so am I."

Shumway looked at him. "You're trapped?"

"By John Chilton's death. He wanted me to continue the fight against the river. If John had been discharged, I could've quit."

"You still can," Shumway said. "But perhaps you're like me — no good at forgetting. And so you'll stay."

Roman nodded, marveling that Shumway should be the one who understood how it was with him. Mohee Jim wouldn't understand it, nor would Angus MacIvor.

Shumway glanced at his watch. "I've a call to make at Lateral Twenty-four," he said, getting up. Then he asked, "Have you seen the Clarion?"

Roman shook his head.

Shumway took a folded newspaper from his hip pocket and handed it over. "Frank Monroe lost no time in transferring his criticism from John to you."

The bold black headline read: "Ben Roman Shanghaies 34 Men!"

"So Monroe is crusading again," Roman mused.

"A born reformer," Shumway said, and went on out of the saloon.

Holding the paper so that it got the light of a nearby bracket lamp, Roman read the story with increasing resentment.

CHAPTER NINE

Clark Hazelhurst stepped off the evening train and was walking past the depot doorway when the night operator handed him a yellow blank. "Weather report for Imperial. Nobody at the office."

Hazelhurst read the brief message: "Hard rains in the San Juans. Green rising."

"Looks like trouble," the operator suggested.

"Did Ben Roman get back from Tucson?" Hazelhurst inquired.

The operator nodded; he asked, "You hear about John Chilton dying?"

"Dying!" Hazelhurst echoed. "Is John Chilton dead?"

"Died of a heart attack this morning. Ben Roman was made general manager in his place."

"No!" Hazelhurst exclaimed. "That can't be!" For a moment he just stood there peering at the telegrapher. Then he demanded, "Are you sure about it? Was there an official notification?"

"A telegram from Ronald Florsheim."

Hazelhurst shook his head as if dazed. "I still can't believe it," he muttered.

"Well, everybody knew Chilton had heart disease," the operator said. "He had a bad seizure a couple of months ago."

"It's not that," Hazelhurst said impatiently. "Why should they make Ben Roman general manager?"

"Seems a trifle odd," the operator agreed.

"Why, it's the most ridiculous thing I ever heard of!"

Hazelhurst picked up his valise and walked along the dark street toward Lacey's Restaurant. Why, he wondered dazedly, had headquarters done such a witless thing? It didn't seem possible. Not after the talk he had made to the board of directors; an inspired talk that had obviously impressed them. The chairman of the board had said quite frankly that his criticism and suggestions would be given every consideration; that he might be chosen to replace Chilton if the general manager were dismissed.

Yet now they had given the appointment to a man who was no more than a fair-to-middling construction boss. It didn't make sense.

Coming abreast of the Weekly Clarion's lamplit doorway, Hazelhurst saw Frank Monroe sitting at a paper-littered desk. "Did you get the particulars about Chilton's death?" Hazelhurst inquired.

Monroe motioned for him to come inside. "No, but I obtained considerable information about Chilton's successor," he said, and handed Hazelhurst a copy of the Clarion. "That, I think, is the best piece of writing I've done in a long, long time."

Hazelhurst glanced at the headline. "Thirty-four men," he mused. He sat on a corner of the desk and read:

Ben Roman, with his armed assistant, Jim Brimberry, arrived in Deseronto today with thirty-four men who gave every indication of being captives. According to Brimberry, the thirty-four unfortunates had been picked up in Tucson, Gila Bend, and Yuma, and were forced to remain on the train. One of them, a man named Moynihan, was severely beaten by Ben Roman when he attempted to escape; so brutally slugged, in fact, that it took a physician to revive him. While this newspaper agrees that Imperial Development has a drastic need for laborers, it does not approve of Roman's recruiting methods and is confident that all right-thinking citizens will join in denouncing such brutality. We are sure that John Chilton, were he alive, would not sanction Roman's tactics. This newspaper is at a loss to understand why the office of general manager wasn't given to someone more fitted for so important a job; Clark Hazelhurst, for instance, who has the welfare of the Valley at heart. It appears that the company has committed another blunder that must be added to a long series of makeshift methods.

Hazelhurst put down the paper. He said, "I appreciate your mention of me, Frank, and I feel the same way about Roman's appointment. It comes as quite a shock to me. When I left Los Angeles it was pretty well agreed by the board of directors that I would replace John Chilton. He must've talked them into appointing Roman instead."

"An unfortunate decision for us all," Monroe said. "Ben Roman just isn't the man for so big a job. He evidently realizes it himself, for he got drunk soon after the news came in. When George Frayne went into the saloon to ask him a question, Roman threatened to cut off his ears. The man is showing his true colors."

Hazelhurst nodded. "I've done all I can," he said. "The Los Angeles office knows how bad conditions are here. I told them that the settlers have reached the end of their patience." He picked up his valise and said, "I don't like to criticize a dead man, Frank, but John Chilton bungled this project from the start."

Then Hazelhurst stared at Ben Roman, who walked through the front doorway.

"You mealy-mouthed bastard!" Roman said. He was bareheaded, one lock of black hair falling across his perspiring forehead. "I warned you," he said, and came on with both fists cocked.

"No fighting in here!" Frank Monroe protested.

Roman laughed at him. "Maybe I'll wreck this goddamn scandal sheet, and you with it," he announced. "But Hazelhurst comes first."

"You're drunk," Monroe said. "Drunk and disorderly."

Roman grinned as he moved forward. He said, "Well, I'm disorderly," and lunged toward Hazelhurst. He swung and missed as Hazelhurst ducked around behind the desk.

"I've got an important message for you," the land agent said. He took the weather report from his shirt pocket and held it across the desk. "There's high water up north, Ben. We're threatened by another flash flood."

"To hell with that," Roman muttered, stuffing the yellow blank into his pocket. "I told you not to put the blame on John Chilton."

"Only did my duty to the settlers," Hazelhurst insisted.

Roman jumped onto the desk and poised there for a moment as the land agent backtracked along a type case. He said, "John gave his life for those goddamn settlers."

Then he leaped in a flying tackle that smashed Hazelhurst against the wall. He cuffed him with both hands; he stepped back for a full swing.

Holding the valise as a shield, Hazelhurst attempted to dodge past Roman. He lost his hat and his blond hair fell like yellow wings on both sides of his face. Using a shoulder against Roman, he tried to barge past, then backed in hasty retreat.

"You can't blame me for Chilton's death," he said frantically. "I had nothing to do with that."

Roman drove Hazelhurst into a corner. He grasped his shirt and was drawing back his fist for a deliberately measured blow when Frank Monroe came in from behind, clutching his arm and pulling him away from the land agent.

Roman turned on Monroe. "So you want in," he snarled, and slugged him with a left to the belly.

Monroe loosed a shrill bleat. His cheeks went chalky, but he clung to Roman's right arm with both hands while Hazelhurst clouted Roman with the valise. Roman whirled away from the desk, dragging Monroe with him. He stopped, picked up Monroe, and carried him to the doorway. Ignoring Monroe's frantic efforts to escape, Roman swung the frail publisher like a sack. He counted, "One, two, three," and flung him out to the sidewalk.

Roman turned as Monroe's body thudded against the plank walk. He saw the high-swung chair and tried to dodge it, and knew there wasn't time.

The chair struck him on the head. He took a teetering backward step and stood propped against the doorframe. He was remotely aware of a tremendous sound that was like the racketing echo of canyon-trapped thunder. He blinked his eyes and wondered why the floor was tilting toward him. He put out a hand to protect his face.

The boards smashed against his hand and against his face. There was a smell of dust, and the faint rumor of far-off voices. And then there was nothing at all.

Dr. Lee Farnum ate a late and leisurely supper at Lacey's Restaurant. She had introduced herself to Slim, saying that she intended to set up practice in Deseronto. Now, finishing her meal, she asked, "Do you think the town needs another doctor?"

Slim shrugged, wondering if so young and pretty a woman could be a capable physician. "We probably wouldn't need another," she said finally, "if Doc Shumway spent less time at the saloon."

"Is he a drunkard?"

"Well, he drinks."

"So that's it," Lee Farnum murmured. "And he's a personal friend of Ben Roman."

Slim shook her head. "Ben hasn't much use for him."

"Oh, you're wrong about that," Lee Farnum said. "You must be."

"Why?"

Lee Farnum took a sip of coffee before saying, "I was hired to replace Dr. Shumway, but Mr. Roman won't have it. He is obviously protecting his friend Shumway."

"Then you've met Ben," Slim said.

"I most certainly have." Lee glanced around, as if making sure they were alone. "In fact, I've been man-handled by him."

"Man-handled?"

Lee nodded, and as Slim stared at her in disbelief, she said, "In case you haven't already found out, Ben Roman is a brute in more ways than one."

"You mean with women?"

"Especially with women."

"I don't believe it," Slim said flatly. "I think you're lying."

Temper flashed in Lee Farnum's eyes. "How dare you say that?" she demanded. Then a knowing smile altered her face and she said slyly, "So you're in love with Ben Roman."

Slim shook her head. "It's just that I don't like to hear him run down. Ben is no angel, but he's no brute, either."

"A matter of opinion," Lee said, appraising Slim now with a fresher interest. "And a matter of comparative values. If you were judging Mr. Roman among a gang of uncouth ruffians, I suppose he would seem less uncouth."

Slim shrugged, having no answer for that. She asked, "More coffee?" and when Lee nodded, she refilled her cup. What, she wondered, had preceded the man-handling this woman talked about? And why had Ben refused to accept her as company doctor?

"I have arranged for a tent in the vacant lot beyond Hoffman's Mercantile," Lee Farnum said. "It will be quite primitive, but at least it's a start in the right direction."

Slim appraised her stylish garb, thinking how tent life would be for a woman accustomed to all the creature comforts of an Eastern city. She said, "It will be quite hot."

"And quite messy," Lee said, "for which I can blame Ben Roman."

Footsteps sounded on the stoop now, and Slim turned to see Frank Monroe open the screen door.

He asked at once, "Have you seen Doc Shumway?"

"Not since suppertime," Slim said. Observing how pale and excited Frank was, she inquired, "Is someone sick?"

"I think Ben Roman's skull is fractured, and I can't find Shumway."

Slim asked urgently, "Where is Ben?"

"At my office. There was a fight, and Clark hit him with a chair."

Hastily taking off her apron, Slim faced

Lee Farnum. "You're a doctor."

Lee nodded, but she made no move to leave the counter.

Slim asked, "Aren't you going to him?"

The lady doctor dabbed at her mouth with a napkin and then wiped her hands, very deliberate about this. She said, "Of course, if I'm needed," and there was a bright shine of anticipation in her eyes as she turned toward the doorway.

CHAPTER TEN

Ben Roman became aware of voices. They were somewhere above him, as if he were lying in a deep, dark well. He had confusing impressions of light and sound that merged with a sensation of pain. There was a long interval when he felt nothing and heard nothing. Afterward a voice said, quite distinctly, "Six stitches."

Roman didn't recognize the voice. He opened his eyes, and blinked them, blinded by lamplight, and closed them again, and heard Slim Lacey exclaim, "He's coming out of it!"

That didn't make sense to Roman. Nor did the fact that he was in bed. Must be dreaming, he thought. But the throbbing ache in his head was no dream. He tried to sleep, and couldn't; presently, as his eyes came into focus, he saw Slim Lacey sitting beside the bed. Her lamplit face was composed and inexpressive as she asked, "How do you feel, Ben?"

Roman thought about that for a moment. He lifted a hand to his bandaged head and moved his head from side to side, grimacing at the reaction. "A trifle on the achy side," he said. "Like I'd been on a God-awful drunk." Glancing about the room, he asked, "How'd I get here?"

"You were toted."

"By who?"

"Frank and Clark."

Roman remembered the fight then. He hunched up on his elbows and swore swiftly at the increased throbbing in his temple. "Hazelhurst put me to sleep," he reflected.

"Be still," Slim cautioned. "Dr. Farnum says you're to stay quiet."

Roman felt of the bandage. "You mean she put this on me?"

"And took six stitches in your scalp."

Roman shook his head and swore again. "Of all the men in Deseronto, I had to be the one who needed a lady doctor," he muttered.

Because Slim seemed so unconcerned about this, he explained, "Lee Farnum was hired by the Los Angeles office. But I wouldn't let her go to work."

"Why not?"

"Well, she's a woman, and it's no job for a woman doctor."

Again Slim asked, "Why not?"

Roman scowled at her. He said impatiently, "You should know that without being told. Suppose she gets called out in a sandstorm, or to go someplace she can't reach in a rig."

"It would be difficult," Slim agreed. Her

eyes were steadily appraising as she said, "Dr. Farnum doesn't approve of you, Ben."

"I know. She thinks I'm a brute."

"Why should she think that?"

Roman peered at her in frank puzzlement. "What's the idea of asking me all these questions? What difference does it make what Lee Farnum thinks of me?"

Slim shrugged. "I'm just curious. Aren't all women supposed to be curious?"

"Well, it started on the train when I had a fight with Black Mike Moynihan. He just wouldn't quit, and I had to hit him pretty hard. Then when she came in and asked where her office was and got uppity about it, I told her to get out."

Slim smiled, wholly pleased with the explanation. "So that's it."

"That's what?"

"Just something I wondered about," Slim said. "I'll get you a cup of coffee."

Roman eased back on the pillow. This, he decided, was Joe Lacey's room, and he wondered where Slim's father was sleeping. He heard someone come into the restaurant, and identified Frank Monroe's voice. Recalling how he had flung the newspaperman out of his office, Roman grinned. Monroe wasn't much of a man, but he had saved Hazelhurst from a beating.

As Slim came in with a cup of coffee, Roman asked, "What did Monroe want?"

"Just asked how you were."

"Probably hoped I was dead," Roman said. "He's another one who doesn't approve of me."

Slim watched him drink the coffee. His black shaggy hair was tousled, giving him a boyish appearance that she had first observed while he lay unconscious on the floor of the Clarion office. It was the first time she had ever seen him wholly relaxed, and his face had been so pale she'd thought him dead. Color had come back into his cheeks now, emphasizing the smoky gray of his eyes. It occurred to Slim that she had never considered Ben handsome, but he seemed so to her now.

"That really hit the spot," Roman said, his grin revealing how much better he felt.

"I'll get you another, while it's hot," Slim offered.

Roman watched her walk out of the room, liking the effortless way she moved. One lock of dark brown hair had come loose from the bun, making a sooty shadow against the smooth column of her neck; that, combined with the sleeveless blouse she wore and the gentle, rhythmic motion of her hips roused an appetite in him that had nothing to do with coffee. All woman, he thought.

Slim brought him another cup of coffee. She sat on the edge of the bed and reported, "Frank was quite worried about you. So was Clark."

"A loco affair, all around," Roman said, and sampled his coffee. "My two worst enemies tote me to a bed, and I'm doctored by a lady medico I wouldn't hire."

Finished with the coffee, he set the cup on a commode beside the bed and asked, "Where's your dad sleeping?"

"He's gone. Left for Oregon the same day you went to Tucson."

Roman thought instantly: Then we're alone, and felt an increasing awareness of her.

"It seems strange, him being away," Slim said. "I can't get used to it."

There was an undertone of regret in her voice. She looked forlorn and resigned, like a woman who'd been forsaken.

"He'll come back," Roman predicted. "When the birds fly south next Fall, Joe will follow them."

Slim shrugged. "It's the first time we've been apart since I can remember."

There was a throaty, low-toned quality in her voice that pleased and stirred Ben Roman. Leaning forward, he put an arm around her shoulders and used his other hand to turn her face so that he could look into her eyes. He said, "Well, you've still got me, Slim."

The misty brightness of unshed tears was in her eyes. He glimpsed a womanly warmth that glowed briefly and was replaced by something else — by an expression that was like questioning, or doubting.

"Have I?" she asked.

The flat disbelief in her voice puzzled Ben Roman. It was as though she had lowered the shield of her self-reliance for one brief moment and now raised it as a barrier between them. He drew her tight against him; he said, "I'm here, aren't I?" and tried to kiss her.

But Slim used her hands against him. She said, "You should be lying down, Ben. Doctor's orders."

"Alone?" he asked with frank disappointment.

"Of course," Slim said, smiling in spite of herself.

Roman was easing back on the pillow when Angus MacIvor hurried in from the restaurant. "Just got word there's high water coming!" he announced, his face flushed and perspiring.

Roman stared at the chief engineer. But he wasn't seeing Angus; he was seeing a rumpled slip of yellow paper, and remembering Clark Hazelhurst's words: "We're threatened by another flash flood."

And that had been hours ago. . . .

CHAPTER ELEVEN

Dr. Shumway sat beside the cot where Agnes Elmendorf lay stricken with typhoid fever. There was little he could do. The prescribed treatment consisted of cold baths to check fever, and stimulation for a failing heart. His black satchel contained the necessary stimulant — a bottle of whisky. But the water from Gus Elmendorf's dug well was lukewarm. A burlap sack, kept moist enough so there was evaporation, had been tacked across the shack's west window; that, and a dampened sheet over the patient, produced a slight cooling effect, which was as near to a cold bath as Doc could devise.

Hattie Elmendorf came in with a wet sheet to replace the one that had dried. She watched Shumway take her little girl's pulse. She waited for him to speak, and when he didn't she asked, "How is her heartbeat, Doctor?"

"No change," Shumway said.

Mrs. Elmendorf's lamplit face was drawn tight with apprehension as she went out to the kitchen, and presently Doc heard her sob, "Please, God, don't let my little girl die!"

Doc remembered the last time he had

prayed. The night Rosalea passed away. It hadn't made any difference, and after that there was nothing to pray for. He watched his little patient, observing how relaxed she was in sleep; how helpless. Rosalea had looked like that in her coffin. Like a little girl sleeping.

Shumway picked up his black satchel and went out to where Gus Elmendorf stood beside the west window with a bucket of water, patiently hand-dousing the burlap. He had come to the Valley six months ago, an eager, ambitious young man wanting a home in this new land and willing to work hard for it. Now his shoulders sagged, and his moonlit face was old with worry.

"I think she'll be all right until morning," Shumway said. "Nothing we can do but wait."

"Wouldn't it be better for you to stay, in case she should take a turn for the worse?"

Shumway shook his head. "I've got to warn folks to boil their drinking water, or we'll have an epidemic on our hands. Other wells may have been polluted."

"The flood," Gus muttered bitterly. "It washed out my crops and now it's given Agnes the typhoid fever."

"An act of God," Shumway said. "A thing that couldn't be helped."

"The company should have built a stronger gate," Elmendorf said. "The flood was not an act of God. It was the result of faulty construction."

"But John Chilton did the very best he knew how. You know that, Gus. No man ever tried harder than John Chilton."

Elmendorf nodded agreement to that. He said, "I'm not blaming him, poor man. Nobody blames Chilton. It's his chief engineer we blame, and Ben Roman, who constructed the gate, and Clark Hazelhurst, whose big promises brought us here in the first place. A green and glorious paradise, his advertisements called it — a magic place where a poor farmer could get prosperous with three harvests."

He jabbed a thumb toward the moonlit wreckage of his fields. "But all we harvest is mud. And now the typhoid fever."

"It has been bad," Doc admitted. "But perhaps the next intake gate will hold against the river, and there'll be no more floods."

He walked over to his rig and got into it and said, "I'll be back sometime tomorrow morning."

Half an hour later Doc approached the Borgstrom place, where lamplight shone faintly through a lilac trellis that formed a leafy ramada in front of the combination board and canvas shack. This was probably the poorest farm in the Valley, being run by widowed Karen Borgstrom and her fourteen-year-old son, Jan; yet now, as he saw lace curtains at both front windows and the flower beds beneath them, the thought came to Shumway that it was the most homelike.

Karen Borgstrom came out as Doc drove into the yard. Standing there with a breeze-blown gingham dress drawn snug against her body, she made a tall and resolute shape. Moonlight burnished her braided hair, giving it a wheat-straw shine that emphasized the tan of her high-boned cheeks.

"Is it Dr. Shumway?" she called, and seeing that it was, said with frank pleasure, "There is still coffee in the pot."

"Can't spare the time," Shumway said, and told her about Agnes Elmendorf. "Don't drink water that hasn't been boiled," he cautioned. "How is Jan?"

"He is fine. Asleep now. He gets so tired, trying to do a man's work. But he is fine."

Again, as it had each time they met, her voice reminded him of Rosalea's. There was the same rich emotional quality in it, and she had a way of looking at him, half smiling, as if in admiration. It was an odd thing. Karen Borgstrom, who worked in the fields like a man, possessed a self-reliance that was in direct contrast to Rosalea's dependence. Yet this sturdy blonde woman reminded him of Rosalea. . . .

"I will go over and help Mrs. Elmendorf tomorrow," Karen said. "She will be up all night with Agnes."

"Aren't you afraid of catching typhoid?"

She smiled at him. "Are you?"

"Well, no. I'm too old to catch anything."

"Then we are alike," she said, "and we have no fear."

"But you're not old," Shumway protested.

Karen laughed at him. "Old as you, Doctor." After a moment she added, "Sometimes I am also lonely, like you."

"How would you know I'm lonely?"

Karen shrugged. "There is an old Swedish saying that there is but one loneliness worse than a man without a wife."

"What's that?"

She smiled at him again, and shook her head. "It would not be fitting for me to say, Doctor."

Shumway thought about it as he drove from the yard. What loneliness could be worse than that of a man living by himself; a man who'd lost the wife he worshiped?

Karen Borgstrom seemed to know, but wouldn't tell him.

Abruptly then the answer came to him, and he said thoughtfully, "A woman without a husband."

The significance of it shocked Shumway. He had been pleasantly aware of the fact that Karen Borgstrom treated him with more respect than most folks showed, but it had never occurred to Doc that she might have romantic notions. She was, he'd thought, wholly self-reliant, a tranquil, easy-smiling woman whose composure and cheerfulness never varied; a mother whose whole interest and affection were centered on her boy. But Karen had spoken of a loneliness that was kindred to his own; the loneliness of a woman who had lost her husband.

He thought: She knows what I am.

Yet she had spoken.

Thinking back to the scene in the dooryard, Doc recalled how she had looked, standing there in a wind-whipped dress. He had not thought of her as being voluptuous; but now, understanding how it was with her, he realized that Karen Borgstrom had been something more than a tall and resolute shape in the moonlit yard. She was a warm, full-blown woman with a woman's needs.

Afterward, dreading the long drive ahead of him, Doc took a bottle of whisky from his satchel. "At least six hours of travel," he muttered, "which means six drinks." Holding the bottle up to examine its contents, Doc wondered if the whisky would last out the night.

CHAPTER TWELVE

The first streamers of sunrise were tinting the eastern sky when Ben Roman drove a buckboard into the construction camp at Pilot Knob. Three teams hauled the light wagon, and a saddled horse was tied to its tail gate; behind this came another three-team rig with Angus MacIvor at the reins and farther back were four wagons piled high with sandbags, hay, grain, and provisions.

Only the camp cook was up, a rheumy-eyed old man who stood in the cook-shack doorway with a skillet in his hand. "How many more for breakfast?" he asked sourly.

"Six," Roman said, driving on toward the corral.

Mohee Jim Brimberry had been sleeping in a wagon; he got up now, tousle-haired and grumpy. "What you doin' here at this time of day?" he demanded.

"High water coming at us," Roman announced, untying his horse and stepping into the saddle. "Roust out Caruso and Moynihan."

Riding toward the river, Roman was aware of an odd sense of insecurity. It was like dizziness; like being drunk and unable to main-

115

tain proper balance. His head throbbed in rhythm to the bay gelding's shuffling gait. Lifting his hat, he fingered the sore place on his scalp and felt the stitches. Slim Lacey had warned him against making this trip; she had said he should remain quiet for at least another day.

Roman thought: I've felt worse and lived. Felt worse and worked, too.

He rode to the north end of what had been MacIvor's intake gate. Observing the twisted piling and battered timbers, Roman remembered how indestructible the massive structure had appeared, how permanent. Silt-laden water, brown as liquid chocolate, lapped at the sanded opening. The broad shallow river made a softly sighing sound; it seemed wholly peaceful and contained.

MacIvor came up the embankment and asked, "How you feel?"

"Well, I'm still breathing."

"Go over to the bunkhouse and take it easy," MacIvor said. "I'll yell if you're needed."

Roman shook his head. He asked, "How many loads of rock will it take to support a barrier dam that will hold?"

Angus squinted at the flood-gouged opening, estimating its length. "Upwards of a hundred, and that may not be enough."

"It better be," Roman muttered.

During the next hour, while men ate hurried breakfasts, Roman made his assignments. Caruso's crew would assemble plank shoring and place it against piles already being driven to MacIvor's instructions. Black Mike Moynihan's big gang was split into teamsters and loaders, with Mohee Jim Brimberry handling the fresno crew. Most of the new workers received the news of an impending flood with disbelief.

How could there be high water without rain, without even a cloud in the sky as far as the eye could see? It made no sense to them. But Caruso's men understood; they kept a wary watch on the river as they worked. This intake channel could be a death trap.

Roman remained at the intake with MacIvor while the shoring operation got under way. He also kept a wary watch on the river, gauging its imperceptible rise by the watermark on a pile. He tilted the brim of his hat against the sun's horizontal glare and urged Caruso's men to increase their efforts.

MacIvor, pessimistic as always, asked, "Suppose we get a barrier in before the flood hits us? It'll take a month to clear it out and build a new gate that'll give diversion. What'll the settlers do for water all that time?"

Roman shrugged. "First things first, Angus. One more flood might wash Imperial out of existence."

"Be a blessing," MacIvor muttered. Then, as a barge came across the river with a huge brush mat in tow, he shouted, "Upstream, you fools!" and waved directions for its placement.

A four-horse hitch scrambled up the west embankment dragging a pair of long piles. The teamster, expertly swinging the leaders, maneuvered the piles so that they rolled free of the shoring crew. When he struck up a conversation with Caruso, Roman called, "No time for visiting, boys. We're pressed for time."

He peered back along the levee to where a rising cloud of dust signaled the movement of many teams. He estimated the hours it would take to haul a hundred loads of rock and wondered if it could be accomplished before high water came. Presently he rode toward the rock dump, which was at the end of a railroad spur near the main line. The throbbing in his head got worse, and he thought of going to the cook shack for a cup of coffee, but there wasn't time.

When he met the first wagon, Roman hailed the teamster, urging, "Hustle those horses, friend. Hustle them!"

All along the dust-veiled road he rawhided teamsters to faster traveling. When a man protested that his team would be worn out in one day, Roman said impatiently, "We've got more horses than we've got time."

He rawhided himself also. He thought: A night shift might've made the difference. He cursed, thinking of the wasted hours.

Black Mike Moynihan acknowledged Roman's arrival at the rock dump with the reluctant civility of a man showing more respect than was necessary. He was still a trifle on the achy side, Roman supposed, and felt a sense of kinship. They had both lost a fight and were feeling the effects of the battering they'd received. Roman watched the loaders, observing that these men were doing an adequate job. But they weren't hurrying.

He said, "Caruso's crew is outworking yours, Mike."

"The hell you say."

Roman nodded. "Seems odd, but it's a fact."

He watched three wagons being loaded simultaneously. It occurred to him that these workers wouldn't be here except for the shanghai deal Frank Monroe had criticized, and that there would have been no chance to build a barrier dam without them. He balanced that against the wasted hours last night and felt less guilty.

The sun had a bite to it now, and men's shirts were showing sweat stains. Roman said to Moynihan, "Maybe you should go ask Tony how he does it."

"Me, ask that Eyetalian?" Moynihan demanded. "Me, Michael Seamas Moynihan,

that ran the best gang on the whole goddamn Union Pacific railroad? What kind of
malarky are ye handin' out? The man don't
live that can tell me how to get work out of
a gang."

Roman shrugged. "Tony's crew is outworking yours."

He rode away from the dump then,
keeping his horse to a walk until he heard
Black Mike bellow, "Come on, ye stinkin'
laggards!" And presently, looking back,
Roman observed that Moynihan was on the
dump himself, heaving rock into a wagon.

By ten o'clock Pilot Knob was a scorching
hell of heat and dust and seeming confusion.
Teamsters cursed sweat-lathered horses in a
continuous shuttle of wagons and fresnos;
perspiring laborers heaved rock and dirt and
sandbags in a constant effort to keep the fill
above steadily rising water. Men needed no
urging now. The river was up eight inches
and flowing faster. Its voice had been a
whisper at dawn; now it spoke with an increasing rumble.

Roman ranged the long barricade, directing
the work, consulting with MacIvor and two
assistant engineers. He was cursing a careless
teamster whose wagon had tipped over when
Clark Hazelhurst arrived with a telegraphic
report of high water in the Gila.

Roman read the message in frowning silence. This first rise, then, was from a flash

flood the Gila had dumped into the Colorado above Yuma.

"I'm sorry about last night," Hazelhurst said, very sober and sincere in the way he spoke. "I shouldn't have hit you with that chair. But I still think you had no right to jump me as you did."

Roman shrugged, and now Hazelhurst asked, "Are you going to make it in time, Ben?"

"Depends on how much time we have."

Hazelhurst glanced toward the river, observing its rolling flow. He said, "Folks in Deseronto are worried. They think another flood will wash the town away." When Roman ignored that announcement, the land agent said in a mildly censuring voice, "They're complaining because you cleaned out the company's supply of sandbags."

"To hell with them," Roman muttered, and looked at Tony Caruso, who came running across the rock fill.

"Fred Pratt is bad hurt!" the little foreman reported.

"What happened to him?"

"The piles, they roll over him," Caruso said, his swarthy sweat-greased face tight with the horror of what he'd seen. "Both legs are crush!"

Roman cursed, and now, as two men carried Pratt toward the bunkhouse, he turned to Hazelhurst. "How about you taking him to Deseronto?"

"I came horseback," the land agent said, "but I could make a fast ride and send Doc Shumway back."

Roman considered that suggestion in frowning silence for a moment. It might take a trifle longer, but the injured man would be better off in bed than bouncing around in a wagon. "Do that," he said. "Tell Doc to come on the run."

As Hazelhurst hurried toward the corral, Roman said to Caruso, "If there's whisky in camp, douse some on Pratt's legs and give him the rest to drink."

Water was lapping at the low spots in the barricade at noon when Angus MacIvor announced, "Up four inches in the past hour, Ben. That's faster than our fill is going in."

Roman peered into the dust haze west of the intake, appraising the progress of on-coming wagons. "The bastards are lallygagging again," he muttered. Going down the embankment to where his horse was tied, Roman got into the saddle and loped to the first wagon. "Shake 'em up!" he shouted. "Use your whip!"

And now, as an empty wagon came off the embankment, he told the driver, "Trot your team, friend. Don't let those horses walk."

Afterward, when every worker on the job had been asked, commanded, or cursed into increased effort, Roman paid a visit to the injured laborer. Pratt lay propped in a bunk with a bottle of whisky in one hand and a cigar in the other. "Where's that doctor at?" he asked.

"Be here soon," Roman assured him. "How you feel?"

Pratt glanced at his blanket-draped legs. "They was numb, but now they're beginning to hurt awful. The pains shoot all the way up to my hips." He took a swig from the bottle and asked, "Doc won't want to amputate, will he?"

"Why, no. He won't want to. Doctors never like to do that unless there's no other way."

Pratt took another drink. Then he said excitedly, "I'll not let him, by God! He can't cut my legs off, you understand? No matter what happens, he's not to do that."

"Don't worry about it," Roman said.

But hurrying back to the barricade, he wondered if Shumway would have to amputate, and was sickened by the thought.

There was no halt for a noon meal. At two o'clock, with men grumbling for food, Roman began releasing every third teamster with instructions to be back at work in thirty minutes. Soon after that he had Mohee Jim rig up a chuck wagon and haul it to the rock dump so that Moynihan's gang could eat in relays without a complete cessation in the loading.

By three o'clock the barrier dam had been

breached so often that a miniature lake was forming beyond it, a muddy bog through which tired teams plodded in slow-motion misery. The barricade was over six feet high at its lowest point, but the Red Bull lunged at full stride now, a wild rampaging monster whose roar was like constant thunder. Swirling brown water spilled across the barrier, gouging channels that had to be filled quickly with dirt and sandbags; unseen water, seeping through the shoring, bored secret passages that caused sudden cave-ins.

Late in the afternoon a crevasse opened beneath a fresno. The driver fell into the break with his frenzied horses and was trampled by them. His left leg was broken above the knee before Ben Roman could drag him out of the muddy mess. Roman carried him off the barricade, waving back offers of assistance.

"Get the horses out," he ordered, "and fill that hole."

Clear of the dam, he eased the injured man to the ground. "What's your name?"

"Joe," the man said sullenly. "Just Joe."

Roman grinned at him. He said, "Stick your right arm over my shoulder, Just Joe, and use me for a crutch."

They were nearing the bunkhouse when Clark Hazelhurst hurried up and said, "We've got to have help with Pratt. He won't let Dr. Farnum administer chloroform."

"Dr. Farnum?"

Hazelhurst nodded. "I couldn't locate Shumway, and this was an emergency."

Roman cursed. "Did you look for Doc at the saloon?"

"Yes, and at the hotel. He hasn't been in town since day before yesterday. Must be lying drunk somewhere."

Roman helped Joe into the bunkhouse, and was aware of its hospital odor of chloroform and antiseptic. Lee Farnum, who wore a white smock over her dress, watched him escort Joe to a bunk. Except that her cheeks held more color than Roman remembered, she showed no sign of the long hot trip from Deseronto or this room's stifling air.

"Another patient?" she asked calmly.

"Broken leg," Roman said.

He glanced at Pratt, whose legs were now covered by towels to protect them from flies. He asked, "What's the trouble, friend?"

"I ain't taking no chloroform," Pratt muttered.

"Why not?"

"Because she might amputate my legs off and —"

"Nonsense," Lee Farnum broke in. "I've told him there's a good chance I can save his legs. But I must remove damaged tissue in order to set the bones properly, and I can't do that unless he's perfectly still."

Roman walked over to the bunk, feeling sorry for this sweat-drenched man. "You'd better do as the Doctor says."

"I don't want no woman messing with me," Pratt insisted. "I'll wait for Doc Shumway."

Roman shook his bead. "You can't do that. No telling when Doc would get here. Miss Farnum is a good doctor. She'll fix you up if you'll just do as she says."

Pratt shook his head. A wildness came into his eyes and he shouted, "I won't take no chloroform! I'd sooner be dead than have my legs cut off!"

Roman tried to calm him, tried to explain that cutting away the mangled flesh might save his legs. "It should be done right now, before infection sets in," he warned. "Another hour might be too late."

But Pratt, writhing in an agony of pain and fright, refused to listen. "No, no, no!" he whimpered. "I'd sooner be dead!"

Roman looked at Lee Farnum and asked, "Can't you give him something to quiet his nerves? The pain has made him jittery."

"He refuses to take anything," she said, very calm about all this. "He won't let me do anything."

"Perhaps we can hold him still enough for you to do what has to be done," Hazelhurst suggested.

She shook her head. "He can't be treated properly without chloroform. There's too much to be done and it will take too long."

Roman looked down at Pratt. He said,

"I'm sorry, friend," and slugged him on the jaw.

For a moment, as Pratt went limp, Lee Farnum peered at Roman in shocked silence. Then she placed a cone over Pratt's face and handed Hazelhurst a bottle of chloroform. "Just a drop at a time," she directed, and uncovered Pratt's mashed legs.

Roman watched her pluck a scalpel from a pan of hot water. He asked, "You need me any longer?"

She shook her head, and now, as he walked to the doorway, she said, "Thanks. Thanks very much."

Ben Roman didn't look back.

He went quickly around behind the bunkhouse and was sick.

CHAPTER THIRTEEN

Hour after hour the battle at the barrier continued, with fatigue-soured men toiling in obedience to a boss who would not quit. When darkness came three huge bonfires were lighted, their fitful illumination transforming the dust haze into a scarlet fog through which the weirdly distorted shadows of men and wagons moved in a thunderous realm of unreality.

Although Ben Roman did not visit the rock dump again, he knew by the continuing arrival of loaded wagons that Black Mike was working his gang to the limit of human endurance; and the returning empties told Moynihan that Roman hadn't surrendered to the Red Bull.

"A bold one, that Roman," Mike told his men. "Must be some Irish blood in his veins."

Lee Farnum expressed a similar opinion while eating a late supper with Clark Hazelhurst in the cook shack. She said, "There's a wild pagan strain in Ben Roman that gives him the courage to do what has to be done. You must give him credit for that, Clark. He has courage."

"Sheer brutality," Hazelhurst said. "That's what he used on Pratt, and it's what he's using out there at the dam."

"Perhaps, but it gets results," Lee Farnum said. "How else could Pratt have been handled? And is there a nice, gentlemanly way of fighting a flood-swollen river?"

Hazelhurst conceded the point by asking, "But why should you defend him?"

"I'm not, Clark. I'm merely attempting to understand him." She smiled, adding, "His type is new to me. I've met educated men who were ruthless or domineering or mean. Clever, dangerous men." She eyed him thoughtfully for a moment. "Who use their minds and their manners to influence people and to get what they want."

"You have sharp eyes," he said mockingly.

"Sharp enough to understand that you want to be general manager of Imperial Development," she said. "Sharp enough to guess you've convinced Frank Monroe that you're a martyr whose only thought is for the unfortunate settlers." She smiled at him, wholly gracious. "I'm not criticizing you. I'm merely saying that I've met your type before. But never a man like Ben Roman. He's so — Well, he makes brutality seem natural."

Hazelhurst chuckled, enjoying this. "The West has plenty of men like Ben. You'll find them in cow camps and mining towns from Mexico to Montana. They're a typical breed, having no ambition to be more than they are. A reckless, careless breed. Educated toughs bossing ignorant toughs."

He reached over and took her hand, caressing it. He said, "I've never met a woman like you, Lee. So accomplished, and so beautiful."

"Why, how nice of you to say that," she murmured and smiled at him as she retrieved her hand. "It's good for us to have someone around we understand so well."

Hazelhurst winced. "I didn't say you were transparent," he objected. "It's not nice for you to say I am."

Lee laughed at him. She said, "Let's not try to fool ourselves, Clark. We're both ambitious. We want certain jobs and will do almost anything to get them."

"Well, you're blunt enough about it," Hazelhurst said.

"Perhaps there's a strain of brutality in me, too."

Hazelhurst shook his head. "Not brutality. The strain is much more refined and enjoyable."

He held up his empty cup and called to the cook, who stood in the doorway, "I'll have another cup of coffee, please."

"Pot's on the stove," the old man said, not turning around. "I ain't runnin' no stylish café."

Hazelhurst shrugged and went to the stove.

When he came back Lee Farnum asked, "I wonder what Ben Roman would do in a case like that."

"Threaten to kick his teeth out, most likely."

Lee thought about it for a moment. Then she said, "No, I think Roman would have waited on himself in the first place."

"Course he would," the cook agreed, and spat disgustedly.

At midnight, with water seeping over the barricade in a dozen places, the barrier dam seemed doomed. The men were dead on their feet, the teams worn out. The river's strength had increased with each passing hour, and now it hurled its hardest blows at the water-sogged barricade.

Angus MacIvor came wearily across the dam to where Roman stood. "We're licked," he announced. "Just a matter of minutes now."

Roman peered at flame-burnished floodwater that smashed against the barrier in unceasing assault. The gleaming silt-laden rollers were like an endless herd of stampeding cattle roaring out of the night's blackness.

"Call it quits!" MacIvor urged. "This whole shebang will bust wide open!"

Roman shook his head. He muttered, "Let it bust," and turned to curse a laggard laborer who had stopped to roll a cigarette, "You can smoke tomorrow," he shouted. "Tonight you work!"

Soon after that Roman was astonished to see Lee Farnum come toward him through the dust-hazed firelight. She held out a cup of coffee and said, "Cook told me you had no supper."

She had to shout in order to be heard above the river's roar, yet she sounded quite calm and assured.

Roman took the coffee. He asked, "You changed your mind about me, Doc?"

Lee shook her head. "But you're holding back the river, and I think it's marvelous."

She gestured at the activity, the shadowy shapes of men and horses toiling in dust-hazed firelight. "There's something so vital about this. So elemental. Men against the elements."

Her enthusiasm and the hot coffee combined to banish the futility that had clawed at Ben Roman's confidence all this night. He grinned at her in frank admiration and finished the coffee while she waited. Handing back the empty cup, he asked, "How is Pratt?"

"Fine," she shouted. "He'll keep his legs."

Roman leaned over so that his mouth was close to her ear. He said, "That's marvelous too." The feminine scent of her hair was intoxicating. Her eyes, masked by the sooty shadow patterns of long lashes, were mysterious and alluring. He savored her fragrance; he said, "Marvelous and elemental."

There was this moment while they remained unmoving and attentive in the fitful glow of barricade bonfires, a moment of frank appraisal and silent speculation; a moment of mutual awareness, old as caves. . . .

Then Angus MacIvor rushed up to Roman and grasped his arm and shouted, "The south end is going out!"

Roman whirled, saw the vague shapes of terror-stricken men scampering from the barricade. As a teamster attempted to turn back with a load of sandbags, Roman yelled, "No! Go on — go on!"

As the teamster jumped off the wagon, Roman ran toward it. Gaining the seat, he drove toward the flooding breach.

Lee Farnum watched him tool the wagon close to the river side of the dam. When he began throwing sandbags into the breach she turned to Angus MacIvor and exclaimed, "How wonderful!"

"He's crazy," MacIvor said. "Crazy and mule-stubborn."

Then he walked reluctantly toward the wagon.

Other men, whose shame was greater than their fear, returned to join Roman in his frantic effort to hold back the river. They cursed him; they cursed the river, and the day they were born. But they went back to the barricade.

It took an hour to close the breach, a nightmarish hour while MacIvor, Caruso, and Brimberry worked shoulder to shoulder with Roman. An hour of grunting, panting, sweat-soaked struggle, after which they stood in the slumped and silent fashion of men beyond the power of speech. When an assistant engineer reported a drop in the river and predicted that the flood's crest had passed Pilot Knob, there was no cheering, no jubilance. They were that tired.

Ben Roman dug out his Durham sack and passed it to the man he had cussed out for stopping to roll a cigarette. He said, "It's tomorrow, friend. Have yourself a smoke now."

There was another battle that night. It was fought in quiet desperation by a tired doctor who watched his patient surrender to an opponent more relentless than the river. It ended at dawn with Gus Elmendorf attempting to quiet his grief-stricken wife, who sobbed accusingly, "You've let her die! My little girl is gone!"

The sound of her wailing followed Doc Shumway as he drove across the flats. It was a dismal chant that ran on and on, like the echo of an echo. Doc opened his satchel and took out the bottle. Only a few drops left. He drank what there was and tossed the bottle away. He was beyond the sound of Hattie Elmendorf's voice now, but he couldn't discard the memory of it. She blamed him for the little girl's death. Her husband blamed the company, but Hattie blamed him.

Doc was thinking about that when he drove into Karen Borgstrom's yard. Mothers invariably accused a doctor when he failed to save a sick child. If the child was critically ill and survived, God got the credit. But if death came, the doctor was blamed.

Young Jan, busy harnessing a team at the shed, called, "Good morning, Doc."

A fine boy, Shumway thought. But thinner than he should be. Eyeing him with a physician's appraisal, Shumway asked, "Do you feel all right, son?"

"Sure," Jan said.

And now Karen came out of the house. She peered at Doc intently, her smile fading. "Agnes is dead?"

Shumway nodded. "Did all any doctor could have done," he said wearily.

"Of course," Karen agreed, and motioned for him to get down. "Come have breakfast, Doctor."

Shumway shook his head. "Only one thing I need now," he said, as if admitting a shameful thing to himself.

"Whisky?"

Doc nodded.

"Then come have whisky," Karen invited. "There is a bottle my husband kept on the top shelf. It has never been opened."

Doc stared at her, shocked by the invitation. In all the years he had been practicing medicine, no woman had offered him whisky. Countless women had criticized him for drinking, even wives whose husbands drank. They could be tolerant and understanding of their own men's drinking, accepting it as a normal weakness. But a doctor was not as other men. He could have no weakness.

Now Karen said gently, "Come, Doctor. The whisky will help you to relax."

CHAPTER FOURTEEN

For three days, while Roman and MacIvor kept a constant watch on the barricade, the river slowly subsided. At noon of the fourth day MacIvor predicted, "At this rate it'll be two weeks before we can start work on a new gate. Maybe longer."

Clark Hazelhurst asked, "And how long after that will it take to get water flowing into the laterals?"

"A month or six weeks, if we're lucky," MacIvor said.

"That's too long for the settlers to wait," Hazelhurst said. "They'll lose what crops the flood didn't wash out. Every farmer in the Valley will be ruined. Isn't there some way that work could be started right now, instead of waiting until the river goes down? Some way you could get diversion within a few days?"

MacIvor shook his head. "Not unless we made a new cut above this one."

"Then why not do that?" Hazelhurst said eagerly.

His fault-finding attitude irritated Ben Roman, who said, "Angus is chief engineer, and he'll do what can be done. Tell your settlers we'll get diversion to them just as soon as it can be accomplished."

"But if a new cut would be faster, why not do it?"

"Because we'd be taking a chance on flooding the whole valley," Roman said. "Suppose we make the cut, and then get hit by another flash flood before the gate is completed?"

MacIvor nodded agreement to that. "We could save a lot of time, if everything went all right. But if a big one came down on us we'd never be able to stop it."

"Aren't you taking that chance anyway?" Hazelhurst persisted.

"Not so big a chance, if we wait until the water goes down."

That settled the argument as far as Ben Roman was concerned. Turning off the barricade, he headed toward camp. Most of the men had gone out to work on the canal, Caruso's gang to repair broken headgates while Moynihan bossed a fresno crew repairing levees. Jim Brimberry was kept busy in the corral, doctoring horses that had been galled or lamed by overwork. He had struck up a friendship with Lee Farnum, conferring with her about treatment for a horse that seemed to be suffering from colic, yet didn't respond to standard treatment.

"She sure knows medicine," he said when Roman stopped by the corral. "That horse would've been a goner if it hadn't been for her. Any fool can doctor humans, but it takes real brains to cure a sick horse."

Mohee Jim wasn't alone in his admiration of the new lady doctor. Fred Pratt, convinced now that he wouldn't lose his legs, fairly worshiped her, and the cook was so impressed by Lee Farnum's presence that he shaved regularly each morning. Judging by the number of men who had shown up at Lee's tent complaining of various ailments, Roman suspected that an epidemic of romantic fever had broken out in camp.

After supper, accompanying Lee to her tent, he asked, "How many heart patients today?"

"Only two that I'm sure about," she reported, smiling. "You'd never guess who one of them was."

"Moynihan?"

"No, Angus MacIvor. He's a dear. I gave him some pills, but what he really needed was a friendly chat with a woman."

"Didn't think he had a speck of romance in him," Roman said.

Lee smiled. "The man doesn't live who hasn't. Some men keep it pretty well concealed. They may not even be aware of it themselves. But it's there. A fundamental ingredient."

Day's heat remained. Dust, stirred up by home-coming crews, still lingered in the windless air. As they passed the lamplit bunk-house a man in the doorway complained, "It's an oven fit for baking bread."

Thinking that the tent was also an oven during the day, Roman asked, "Still think this is the land of opportunity?"

"More so than ever. I've seen what can be accomplished by a man who refused to quit."

"Me?"

She nodded.

A whimsical smile creased Roman's cheeks. "I thought we were licked the other night," he admitted. "It made me madder'n hell."

"And so you kept on fighting," she mused. "That's how it was with me, when I wanted to be a doctor and everyone said a woman shouldn't be one."

"Mule-stubborn," Roman said, and remembered what she had said that first day as she left his office. The day he'd kissed her. " 'I'm going to remain in Deseronto,' " he quoted her, " 'and I'm going to show you what a woman doctor can do.' "

He couldn't see her face clearly in the deepening dusk, but she sounded embarrassed as she said, "I was angry. Angrier than I'd ever been. But I meant it. I'm going to stay, and I'm going to show you."

"I've been shown," Roman said. "You're quite a doctor, Doc. You are for a fact."

"But not good enough to work for Imperial Development."

"Well, maybe I was wrong about that," he admitted.

Lee shook her head. "You weren't wrong, Ben. What you did was right. I thought your refusal was because of friendship for Dr. Shumway. A purely personal thing. If that had been so, you'd have been terribly wrong in doing what you did. But I'm convinced now that it was for what you considered the project's best interests. If that was it, then what you did was right."

Surprised by her tolerant attitude, Roman said, "I just didn't think a woman could handle the job."

"Do you still think that?"

"No. I've seen what you can do."

They were standing in front of her tent now. She waited out a moment of silence before asking, "Then is there a chance for me to have the job?"

"Well, yes. I suppose there is, except that I'd hate to fire Doc Shumway. He's had some tough luck, one way and another. I don't like to hit a man when he's down."

Lee laughed at him. "That sounds odd, coming from you. Didn't I see you slug Moynihan when he was out on his feet? And how about Pratt? Wasn't he down when you hit him?"

Then, not waiting for a reply, she said earnestly, "A man in your position shouldn't be influenced by sentimental considerations,

141

Ben, nor by what happens to individuals. You've got to be above that. You've got to see this project as a great crusade — a magnificent crusade that will benefit the thousands who will come to Imperial Valley. Not just the ones who are here now, but all those to follow. You must see people, not as individuals, but as a great mass of humanity seeking economic advancement."

"Never thought about it that way," Roman said.

"John Chilton must have seen the project like that," Lee said.

Roman nodded. "John thought it was more important than any of the people connected with it, including himself."

"Of course, and that's how you must feel about it, Ben. It's bigger than any of us, or all of us."

She waited out another interval of silence and then asked, "Don't you think I'm right?"

"Suppose so."

"And don't you think I should have the job I was hired for?"

Roman nodded. He said, as if convincing himself, "We'd have been in a bad fix except for you."

"Then I'm on the payroll?" she asked, wanting this definitely understood.

Roman nodded again. "But I'd rather take a licking than fire Doc Shumway," he admitted.

"You are an odd one," Lee murmured, her voice softly intimate. "You didn't hesitate to hit a sick man who needed chloroform, but you don't want to discharge a drunken doctor that headquarters wants to replace. I once called you a brute, Ben, but you're much more complex than that. And much nicer to know."

She came into his arms when he reached for her. She accepted his kiss in the receptive way of a woman savoring passion without sharing it. Afterward she sighed, "Brute Roman."

Early the next morning Lee Farnum and her two patients left for Deseronto in a wagon, the lady doctor smiling acknowledgment as men shouted their farewells. "There," Mohee Jim said, "goes the smartest goddamn female west of the Pecos."

"And the prettiest," Angus MacIvor said.

Roman wasn't sure about her being the prettiest. He had seen some real beauties in this country; Slim Lacey, for instance. But he agreed with Mohee Jim about Lee Farnum's mind. Recalling her talk of last night, Roman thought: She sees this project exactly as John saw it, and he decided that she was right. Individuals weren't important in so big a deal.

That, he supposed, was the explanation of John Chilton's unwavering faith in the project, the reason John had refused to give up.

Being the leader of a "magnificent crusade" was all-important to him; it had dwarfed the loss of his personal fortune and made the ruin of a settler's crops seem unimportant. The thought came to Roman that there was a parallel in Nature, which maintained an impersonal disregard for individual coyote or sparrow or cottonwood tree, yet worked miracles to perpetuate the species. For John Chilton the ultimate and all-important goal had been survival of the project.

Lee Farnum was motivated by a similar philosophy, which seemed reasonable and right. Yet when Doc Shumway drove into camp shortly before noon, Roman had some difficulty convincing himself that individuals didn't count. Doc looked pathetic, getting down from his buggy; he looked tired, and sick, and a trifle ashamed. He brushed dust from the sleeves of his frayed shirt and said, "I hear you had a big fight with the river."

Roman nodded. He thought: The damned counterfeit has been on a toot.

Doc glanced toward the barrier dam. "River gone down?"

"Some," Roman said. "Where you been hiding out?"

"Hiding out?" Shumway echoed.

"Well, nobody could find you these past few days. Hazelhurst searched the town. He even looked in French Nellie's place, thinking you might be there."

Doc gawked at him. "Did Clark think I'd — Why, that's an insult!"

"Well, men have been known to do it, especially with a bellyful of booze."

Doc shook his head. "I've never been that drunk," he said, "and I never will be."

"Where were you, then?" Roman asked.

"I was kept busy at the Elmendorfs, until the little girl died."

"What did she die of?"

"Typhoid."

"That's too bad," Roman said. "She was a cute kid. Must be bad for her folks." Then he asked, "What day was that?"

Doc wasn't quite sure. He nudged back his dust-peppered derby and said, "I guess it was the next morning after I talked to you in the saloon. No, the morning after that. I felt real bad about it. She was such a sweet little thing. And her mother took on something awful, poor soul. When I stopped by Karen Borgstrom's place, she gave me what I needed — a quart of bourbon."

Roman continued to frown. But he felt better about this chore now. "You're all through with Imperial," he announced. "You should've been discharged a long time ago."

Doc Shumway didn't seem much surprised. He said, "They told me in town there was a new lady doctor. Is she going to take my place?"

"She already has. Four days ago. Except for

her, a man would've lost his legs, or maybe died."

Doc started to say something, then changed his mind. He turned to the buggy and climbed into it and sat there for a moment in shoulder-slumped dejection. Then a wistful smile altered his face. He said meekly, "I don't blame you, Ben," and drove off at a slow, plodding walk.

Roman went into the engineers' shack and spent the afternoon with MacIvor, discussing plans for construction of a new intake gate. At suppertime George Frayne arrived with a telegram from Los Angeles:

EXTREMELY URGENT DIVERSION TO LATERALS BE ESTABLISHED FIRST POSSIBLE MOMENT BECAUSE OF IMPENDING LAWSUITS. RECOMMEND HAZELHURST PLAN FOR NEW CUT BE FOLLOWED AT ONCE REGARDLESS OF RISK INVOLVED.

RONALD FLORSHEIM

Roman handed the telegram to MacIvor. "Our nosy land agent has been burning up the wires," he muttered. "Goddamn a man who can't mind his own business!"

Angus read the telegram and handed it back. "Clark has convinced them it should be done."

"But he's not the chief engineer of this

outfit. You are, and if you say no to this proposition, I'll tell Florsheim to go to hell."

MacIvor thought about it in scowling silence for a long moment. Finally he said, "We could get quick diversion. No doubt about that. With the river this high, it wouldn't take much digging. The water would do most of it for us."

"And suppose it rises again, instead of going down?" Roman asked.

"Well, we could build an overhead barrier that might work in case of emergency — a dynamite dam. They're practical for small openings up to a thirty-foot span. After that they're no good at all."

Roman nodded, understanding the limitations of so ponderous a contrivance. He said, "It's up to you, Angus."

"No, by God!" MacIvor protested. "I'm not running this project. I'm just working on it, against my better judgment. I say diversion can be obtained, with some risk. But you're general manager and the decision is yours to make."

Roman said, "Well, on one side we're faced with bankruptcy and on the other we're taking a chance on getting washed out of existence."

"A poor proposition any way you look at it," MacIvor agreed. Then he picked up the telegram and demanded, "What are we fretting about, Ben? The Los Angeles office has

147

ordered us to do it, regardless of risk. The responsibility is theirs, not ours."

"Hazelhurst's," Roman mused. "So we'll give him his quick diversion."

CHAPTER FIFTEEN

Ben Roman's return to Deseronto was the signal for a parade of visitors to the Imperial Building. He had scarcely seated himself at John Chilton's old desk when three members of the citizens' committee came into the office.

Oscar Hoffman, whose plump face had the slightly scorched appearance of a pudding retrieved from a hot oven, acted as spokesman. He said, "We're glad you kept that flood out of the Valley, Ben. It was a real achievement, from what I hear. A personal triumph. The new lady doctor told us about the way you refused to leave the barricade when everyone else ran off — when it looked as if the whole dam was going out. Magnificent, she called it, and we think the same thing."

The rotund proprietor of the mercantile glanced at his two companions for confirmation. They nodded agreement, and Swede Erickson said, "A brave thing to do, driving that wagon right up to the breach."

"A real hazardous thing," Riley Swane said.

The rawboned owner of the Empire Hotel didn't sound overly cordial, though, and neither did Hoffman when he said, "We appreciate what you did, Ben. We think it was a fine thing. But we don't like the way you took all the sandbags to Pilot Knob, leaving us no protection at all."

"Which is the real reason you're here," Roman said. He looked Hoffman in the eye. "You and your goddamn committee fussed at John Chilton all the time. You made life miserable for him. Don't try it on me. I've got just one idea in mind — to lick that river."

"Yes, of course," Hoffman sputtered. "But town folks should be given some consideration."

"Why?" Roman asked. "Why the hell should you get any more consideration than the settlers?"

Hoffman blinked, unprepared for such a question and confused by it. He glanced at Erickson and Swane in turn, and, getting no help from them, said lamely, "Well, the town is important to us. We have our money invested here."

"What do you suppose the settlers have invested, marbles? Most of them have put every dollar they own into seed, along with plenty of sweat. Don't get the idea that you town folks are so important. You aren't. Not to me. Nothing is important except Imperial Development."

Then, observing how deflated Hoffman was, he said, "I took those sandbags because

150

they were needed. I've ordered another supply so there'll be enough for use here and at Pilot Knob."

They accepted that explanation in the uncertain fashion of men deprived of the basis for argument. Erickson said, "Well, that's good," and walked to the doorway with Swane.

But Hoffman wasn't quite satisfied. He said, "From what I hear, it was an awful close thing. Another inch rise in the river would have gone over your barricade. It's just luck we weren't flooded out."

"Luck, hell!" Roman exploded. "It was work. Eighteen hours of hard work!"

Hoffman held up his smooth merchant's palms. "No need to get snorty, Ben. We appreciate what you did."

"Then quit your squawking," Roman said, and gave his attention to the stack of papers on his desk.

Mohee Jim Brimberry came in as the citizens' committee went out. He had heard the talk, and now he said, "This country is crawlin' with faultfinders, Ben. Half of them are goin' to sue the company for floodin' their places with too much water, and the other half are threatenin' lawsuits because they ain't got water enough. What a hell of a way to earn a livin'!"

"For a fact," Roman agreed. He shaped up a cigarette, propped his boots on the desk, and inquired, "How'd you make out with the Cocopahs?"

"Well, my old friend Mingas Charley will send upwards of thirty men to work on the canal. But they won't work on the dam. He says it's bad medicine to tinker with the Red Bull. According to him, the thunder gods are angry and will send big water that will smash every intake gate we build to smithereens. Just goes to show that Injuns got more sense than white men."

"Who said otherwise?" Roman asked. "Did you ever hear of an Indian sweating his guts out raising more corn than he could eat? Or wearing his heart out trying to make a southbound river run northward so some other Indians can plant more corn than they need? Hell, no. He doesn't try to change nature. He goes along with it."

Mohee Jim nodded. "I can remember when there was lots of good grass in this valley at certain times of the year, especially after the river had gone on one of its rampages. There'd be plenty of water holes in the low places where grass growed stirrup-high. After one of them floods it was a cowman's paradise. I remember a man named Benton who had a cow camp near Black Butte and run lots of cattle over there. But look at it now. No damn good for nothin'."

"Go tell Mingas Charley I'll settle for canal

work," Roman said. "I can sure use some more men."

Brimberry sighed, and swabbed his perspiring face with a bandanna. "Swimmin' in sweat when I should be high up in the Mogollones huntin' mustangs," he complained. At the doorway he turned and asked, "How much longer I got to wait on you, Ben?"

"Nobody asked you to wait."

"But I can't make a gather by myself. It takes a pair of good riders to corral them wild ones." He took a plug of tobacco from his pocket and bit off a chew; he maneuvered it from cheek to cheek in the absent-minded way of a man contemplating an important problem. Finally he asked, "Will you come with me the day this outfit goes bust?"

Roman grinned and nodded. "Still convinced Imperial is headed for bankruptcy?"

"Just a matter of time, is all. But it's tough on a man, waitin' for it to happen."

He went out then, walking with a minimum of exertion.

The next visitor was Lew Gallatin. Freshly shaved and smelling of bay rum, the saloon owner handed Roman a cigar. "That was a great thing you did, stopping the flood."

"Sure, but I shouldn't have taken all the sandbags out of town."

Gallatin chuckled. "That's Hoffman for you. Always fretting about what might happen to his store. A born worrier. But not me. I believe in looking ahead to the big days that are coming. This country will grow in spite of anything that happens."

"You sound like Hazelhurst," Roman said dryly. "What are you selling today, in addition to diluted rotgut?"

"I don't sell rotgut," Gallatin corrected. "Only the best whisky available."

"Diluted," Roman said.

George Frayne brought in a requisition for him to sign. When Frayne went back to the general office, Gallatin announced, "I've decided to branch out a trifle, Ben. I'm going to open up a place at your construction camp."

"So?"

"I think a saloon will do all right out there, with fifty customers for a start. And I'll see that you're taken care of."

"How?"

Gallatin gave him a sly smile. "Ten per cent of the profits, as a token of my friendship."

Roman shook his head.

"But that would run into real money over a period of months," Gallatin said.

"Not enough."

Gallatin frowned. "I couldn't go higher than fifteen per cent."

"Still not enough," Roman said.

Gallatin eyed him narrowly. "What do you

expect — twenty-five?"

Roman reached over the desk and stuck the cigar in Gallatin's vest pocket. He said, "You're not going to open a saloon at Pilot Knob."

"Why not?"

"Because I said so. It's bad enough being short-handed, without having a bunch of drunks to contend with."

Temper brightened Gallatin's eyes. He said, "Perhaps I'll open up without your permission," and turned abruptly toward the doorway.

"Sure," Roman called after him, "and I'll rip down your joint the day it's opened."

After that there were five settlers who came in one at a time to present claims for flood damage; meek, tired-eyed men garbed in sweat-stained shirts and bib overalls. They reported that Clark Hazelhurst had referred them to him, and the bills, on ruled notebook paper, bore identical notations: "Seed and labor lost because of badly built control gate." The amounts ranged from $350 to $1,000.

The settlers solemnly accepted Roman's explanation of why Imperial Development couldn't pay damages and remain solvent. When one man remarked morosely that he would have to find a job at day wages, Roman hired him to work at Pilot Knob.

The sixth settler, a big gangling Kansan

named Joe Grimshaw, arrived as Roman was leaving the office for his noon meal. "I'm going to sue the company unless you agree to pay me damages right now," he announced.

"So?"

"You're damned right it's so. I ain't swollerin' the pap you gave them others, Roman. I want cash on the barrelhead."

Roman shook his head. He explained patiently, "If Imperial had to pay damages for flash floods, it would go out of existence tomorrow."

"You'll pay me damages, regardless!" Grimshaw shouted. "Otherwise I'll sue for twice as much!"

"Sue and be damned."

Rage stained Grimshaw's perspiring face. He shook a fist at Roman. "Don't you cuss me out! I ain't takin' lip from no company crook!"

"Get out," Roman commanded.

But Grimshaw, who stood just inside the doorway, said, "Not till I'm ready to go. Not till —"

Roman jabbed his left fist at the big Kansan's belly, then drove a solid right into his face. Grimshaw was off balance and teetering backward as Roman hit him again. The blow knocked Grimshaw through the doorway, but it was his own heel, caught on the edge of the plank walk, that tipped him over.

For a moment he sat there, bewildered.

Frank Monroe hurried across Main Street. He asked, "What's the matter, Grimshaw?" and helped the big man to his feet.

Grimshaw lifted a hand to his nose and looked at the blood on his fingers. He said, "I put in a claim for damages, and Roman beat me up."

"Just for asking damages?" Monroe asked in disbelief.

Grimshaw nodded. He peered at Roman. "You'll pay for this. You'll pay plenty."

"Put it on your bill," Roman said, and walked toward Lacey's Restaurant.

This job, he thought, got worse as it went along. A man could take just so much. He wondered how John Chilton had managed to remain tranquil, never losing his temper, never showing resentment toward his tormentors.

Going into the restaurant, Roman grinned at Slim and said with frank admiration, "Just as pretty as ever."

She poured him a cup of coffee, not speaking until she set it before him. Then she asked, "Roast beef or steak?"

"Beef, served with a smile, if you don't mind."

But she didn't smile, and Roman asked, "Why so serious?"

Slim ignored the question. She served him and went down the counter to make change for a customer. When she came back Roman said, "This town is enough to give a man the running fits."

"Depends on the man," Slim said.

Roman peered at her in growing wonderment. "You sick or something?" he demanded.

Slim shook her head, and now, as Frank Monroe came in, she turned to the coffee urn.

Roman thought: She's sore about something, and wondered what had displeased her.

Monroe took the stool next to Roman. He said, "I've heard Grimshaw's side of the story, Ben. Now I'd like to hear yours."

"So you can write it up in your paper?"

Monroe nodded. "I want to be fair," he said. "There's always two sides to a story."

"Not this one," Roman said. "Grimshaw got mouthy and I hit him. That's all there was to it."

"What did he say?" Monroe asked.

Roman shrugged and went on with his eating. No use explaining the fracas to this newspaper publisher. Monroe wasn't actually seeking his side of it; he just wanted to dig up more dirt for his scandal sheet.

Monroe gave Slim his order, then asked, "Did Grimshaw use abusive language?"

"What difference does it make?"

"I told you I want to write a fair and accurate story."

"Sure," Roman scoffed. "Like that shanghai piece. You didn't ask for my side of that one, did you, Frank?"

Monroe shrugged. "I got my story from your friend Mohee Jim. Surely he wouldn't have given you the worst of it."

"But your paper hasn't mentioned the fact that those unfortunate laborers I brought here saved the Valley from a bad flood," Roman accused. "Not a damn word about that part of it."

"Do you think that makes what you did right?" Monroe asked. "Is building a dam more important than the rights of individuals?"

The mildly derisive tone of his voice irritated Ben Roman. He said, "I think the project is more important than any individual."

"Then you don't think people are important?"

Recalling how Lee Farnum had expressed it, Roman said, "People, yes. All the thousands who will be benefitted in the future. But not Joe Grimshaw, or any other individual."

"Is that how you felt about Doc Shumway when you fired him?" Monroe asked. "Was it for the good of the project?"

"What other reason would I have?"

"I wonder," Monroe mused, and glanced at Slim.

There seemed to be a mutual understanding between them; some shared thought or secret agreement. The sense of it was so strong in Roman that he said, "You think I had some other reason?"

Monroe shrugged. A self-mocking smile altered his thin face. "I won't be maneuvered into a fist fight, Ben. You can outpunch me, but you can't keep me from thinking the truth, or writing it. I'll not be intimidated by your hot temper or the fists that go with it."

Then he asked, "What's this I hear about your refusing to let Lew Gallatin open a saloon at Pilot Knob unless he pays you twenty-five per cent of the profits?"

"Did Gallatin tell you that?" Roman asked angrily.

Monroe shook his head. "I got it from a man who was passing your office doorway. He heard you say that fifteen per cent wasn't enough, and heard Gallatin ask if you expected him to pay twenty-five per cent."

Roman walked to the screen door and opened it. He said, "Think what you like, Monroe. But if you print that in your paper, I'll rub your nose in it."

CHAPTER SIXTEEN

Karen Borgstrom tooled her ranch wagon up beside the blacksmith-shop doorway, where Swede Erickson stood wiping his huge hands on his leather apron.

"So long since you've been in town," he said censuringly. "It is not good for a pretty woman to hide herself on a farm."

Karen smiled and accepted the hand he offered as she got down. This big, kindly man had proposed marriage six months ago, and, failing to impress her as a suitor, now behaved in the way of a privileged friend.

"The bay needs a shoe in front," Karen said. "Jan wanted to do it, but he has not been feeling good these past few days. Have you seen Dr. Shumway today?"

Swede shook his head. "But there is little doubt where he is. Most of his time Doc spends in Gallatin's saloon."

"So?" Karen murmured, revealing no more than casual interest. She watched French Nellie come from the house behind the saloon, observing the stylish clothes this woman wore and wondering how she dared show herself in daylight.

French Nellie smiled at Swede, seeming

not at all perturbed by his barely civil nod. As she passed on along the alley, Karen asked, "What do men see in such a brazen trollop?"

"Well, she has a pleasant, cheerful way," Swede said, a sly twinkle in his eyes. "Sometimes a man likes to have a woman smile at him. Any woman, just so she is pretty."

Karen shook her head. "I see nothing pretty about her." Then she asked, "Has Ben Roman returned from Pilot Knob?"

"Yes, and there is talk the company will go bankrupt. So many lawsuits for flood damage."

"Oh, I hope not," Karen said. Glancing toward the saloon's rear doorway, she asked, "Would you go tell the Doctor I want to see him? Say it is because of Jan."

"Why don't you go see the new lady doctor?" Swede suggested.

Karen shook her head. "I prefer Dr. Shumway."

"Even if he is drunk?"

Karen nodded.

"But they say she is very good, the lady doctor," Swede persisted.

Karen folded her hands. She repeated, "I prefer Dr. Shumway."

Swede shrugged, and, crossing the alley, went into the saloon. He came back alone. "Doc says he is not a doctor any more. He says for you to get Miss Farnum."

Karen frowned. "Is he drunk?"

"Well, he is not sober."

She thought about that for a moment. Then she said, "Please put a shoe on the bay right quick. I'll be back in a few minutes."

She walked tip the alley and quartered across Main Street to the Imperial Building.

Ben Roman was pouring himself a cup of water from the olla when Karen went into his office. He looked angry or irritated, so she said quickly, "I do not like to bother you. I know you are a busy man. But I have come to ask a favor."

Roman looked at her, guessing the favor this tall, tanned woman wanted. He thought: She's got a case on Doc Shumway, and marveled at that knowledge.

"Is it about Doc?"

Karen nodded.

"Well, I had no choice," Roman said. "The Los Angeles office hired Miss Farnum to take his place."

"But you are the general manager," Karen said. "They would listen if you told them how hard the Doctor worked to stop a typhoid epidemic. All night long he drove, from farm to farm, warning people. He would not take time for a cup of coffee."

"Why?"

"Because he had to warn people to boil their drinking water. Even so, there is a case of typhoid at the Van Horns'."

"Well, Doc didn't tell me about warning the settlers," Roman admitted. "I understood he got drunk at your place, on a bottle you gave him."

"Oh, no!" Karen gasped. "The Doctor took only enough to relax his nerves and let him sleep. He was not drunk." She smiled, explaining, "He got so tired. Worn out. And he could not forget how Hattie Elmendorf took on about little Agnes."

"Is Shumway at the Van Horns'?"

Karen shook her head. "The new lady doctor." Then, with utter sadness, she said, "The Doctor is in the saloon."

"Drunk?"

She nodded. "He is so ashamed, being discharged from his job. It made him feel useless. As if there was no need for him. I sent word to the saloon for him to come out, but he will not come. He is too ashamed."

"Doc did plenty of drinking before he got fired," Roman muttered. "It's nothing new."

"I know. He mourned for his wife. That is why he used to drink. He could not forget how young she was. How beautiful. But now it is because he has no job."

She sighed, and waited for him to speak. When he didn't, she said, "Such a shame, just when the Doctor was learning to forget about the past — to think of the future."

"With you?" Roman asked bluntly.

"Perhaps," Karen said, embarrassment

deepening the color of her tanned cheeks. "A month, the Doctor said. If he did not drink for a month we would be married. But the next day you hired the lady doctor to take his place."

"Too bad," Roman said.

Karen nodded. "I came to town, wanting to see you. But you weren't here, so I talked to the lady doctor."

She made an open-palmed gesture that reminded Roman of Slim Lacey. "I said she was young, and could find another place easily. I said it meant so much to the Doctor, and to me."

"What did Miss Farnum say?"

"She was very nice to me. So very nice. But she said it was up to you."

Roman nodded. He thought: What else could she say? "Will you give him another chance?" Karen asked, her eyes frankly pleading.

Understanding how much discarded pride this visit had cost her, Roman felt sorry for Karen Borgstrom. Why, he wondered, should a wholesome, mature woman want a man like Doc Shumway? A pretty, well-made woman who'd been courted by a steady man like Swede Erickson.

Roman shook his head. "I'd like to help him, any other way. If he needs money I'd be glad to stake him."

Karen sighed, revealing neither surprise nor

resentment. She said dully, "I must get the Doctor out of that saloon. My boy is sick. May have typhoid."

"Why don't you stop by at the Van Horns' and ask Dr. Farnum to look at your boy?"

"I want Dr. Shumway," Karen said. She was at the doorway now; she turned and looked at him and asked, "Would you do me that favor?"

"You mean bring him out of the saloon?"

She nodded. "My wagon is at the blacksmith shop. If you would just fetch the Doctor to it —"

Roman grinned. "Be glad to," he said, and reached for his hat.

He felt good, walking into the saloon. This chore was something he could do with his hands; something he could use his strength on.

Doc Shumway sat at a table with a filled shot glass before him. A stubble of whiskers shagged his cheeks, and his eyes were red-rimmed as he looked up at Roman. "Good morning," he said vaguely.

"It's afternoon, Doc, and there's a lady waiting for you at the blacksmith shop," Roman announced.

"The blacksmith shop?"

"Karen Borgstrom. Her boy is sick."

Shumway shook his head. "I'm not practicing," he said thickly. He lifted his glass, spilling a few drops of bourbon. He downed the drink and shuddered. "Pull up a chair and join me, Ben."

"Sure," Roman agreed, "after you talk to Karen."

A wistful smile brightened Shumway's face. "A grand woman, Karen. Best in the world."

He toyed with the empty glass, turning it around and around in his agile fingers. He said, "A woman to warm a man's heart."

"And you shouldn't keep her waiting," Roman said. "Go out back and talk to her."

Shumway shook his head. "Tell her I'm not here, Ben. Tell her I went away. Far, far away."

Lew Gallatin came up to the table with a bottle. "You want another drink, Doc?"

"Yeah," Shumway said. "And bring one for my friend Ben."

"Friend?" Gallatin scoffed. "After the way he gave your job to a pretty blonde?"

Roman elbowed Gallatin aside. "You keep out of this." Grasping Doc's arm, he pulled him to his feet. "Come on out back with me, Doc."

"Why don't you leave him alone?" Gallatin said. "You can't interfere with my customers."

"Can't I?" Roman asked. He got a firm grip on Shumway and propelled him to the rear doorway. "Try and stop me, Lew. Just try it."

Doc had difficulty with his feet. He stumbled and would have fallen except for Roman's support. "You tripped me," he protested. Attempting to pull free, he lost his footing completely.

Roman picked him up and toted him like a sack across the alley to where Karen Borgstrom stood waiting with Swede Erickson beside the wagon. As he deposited Doc on the seat, Karen got quickly up on the other side.

"Jan is sick," she said to Shumway. "We must hurry."

Doc shook his head dazedly, and Roman said to Swede, "Go to the hotel and get his medical kit."

"I've already got it," Karen said. Supporting Shumway with one hand, she picked up the reins. "Thank you, Mr. Roman. Thank you very much."

She drove down the alley.

"Why should she want a drunken doctor for her boy?" Swede Erickson asked.

Roman smiled, guessing how much more bewildered Swede would be if he knew the rest of it. "Perhaps she wants Doc for herself," he suggested. And now, as Swede gawked at him in disbelief, Roman said thoughtfully, "A woman will risk most anything to get the man she wants."

"But why should she want a drunkard?" Erickson demanded.

Roman shrugged, not understanding it himself.

"There is no sense to it," Swede muttered. "She would not marry me. But now you say she wants Doc."

"Maybe it's because he needs a woman to look after him," Roman said, thinking it out as he went along. "Some women are like that."

He thought about it as he crossed Main Street and saw Slim Lacey come out of the mercantile with a basket of groceries. It occurred to Roman that she was like Karen Borgstrom, a woman who had to be needed. He wondered what he'd done that had displeased Slim. Recalling how she seemed to share Frank Monroe's speculation about Doc Shumway's dismissal, Roman thought: They think I did it to make a place for Lee Farnum.

Roman was tempted to overtake Slim, to explain that he'd had no choice in the matter. But a swift-rising resentment made him discard the impulse. A man shouldn't start making excuses to a woman or she'd think she owned him.

Swede Erickson was still standing in front of his blacksmith shop when French Nellie came back along the alley. Stopping beside him, she asked, "Why so glum?"

Swede shrugged. "Women do not make sense," he said.

French Nellie smiled at him. "Some of us

do," she murmured.

The invitation in her eyes was plain enough, and the scent of her perfume reminded Swede of past pleasures. He asked, "You on your way home?"

And when she nodded, he said "I'll stop by after a while."

CHAPTER SEVENTEEN

Four more settlers presented bills to Ben Roman during the afternoon, three of them accepting his offer of jobs at Pilot Knob. By six o'clock, when George Frayne grudgingly admitted there were no more reports to sign or requisitions to approve, Roman said irritably, "If you never have another it will be a month too soon."

He was reaching for his hat when Lee Farnum came in from the street and announced, "I just got back from Lateral Seventeen. Mohee Jim told me you were here."

Aware of his sweat-sogged shirt, Roman marveled that she should look so cool and fresh. He asked, "How do you manage it, Doc?"

"Manage what?"

"To look clean and cool and beautiful after a ten-mile drive in the heat of the day."

She smiled at the compliment. She perched on a corner of his desk and asked, "How are things progressing at Pilot Knob?"

"*Poco a poco,*" Roman said, and seeing that the Spanish phrase meant nothing to her, added, "Little by little. How's the doctor business?"

"There's plenty of it. I've got a case of typhoid, a man with an infected foot, and two pregnancies — all in different directions. We should have some sort of hospital here in town, Ben. Someplace where the sick could be taken care of under one roof."

"Sure," Roman agreed. He tilted back in the swivel chair, his eyes frankly appraising. "Also a concrete intake gate and a water-filtering system, if the company wasn't on the verge of going bankrupt."

Lee shook her head. "I'm not talking about a big, well-equipped hospital. That will come later. But we can make a start — just an ordinary building with a few clean beds, a kitchen, and a practical nurse to take care of things."

"And an office, painted white, for you?" Roman asked amusedly.

"Yes, even if I have to paint it myself. That cubbyhole I've got now is probably crawling with microbes. In fact, I'm sure it is."

Roman chuckled. "Sorry you hired out?"

"Of course not. But I'm serious about the hospital idea, Ben. And I've found a place that can be fixed up with very little expense."

"Where?"

"The tin-roofed storage building beyond the commissary. It has a concrete floor and there's scarcely anything stored there. Just a few odds and ends that could be put in the stable."

172

Roman shook his head. "Mohee Jim would shoot me if I used his horse establishment for storing odds and ends."

"But surely you can find some place for the stuff."

"Suppose," Roman admitted. Observing the increased warmth in her eyes, he thought: It's the hospital, and wondered if a man could rouse her this much.

Clark Hazelhurst came in from the street. Removing his hat and bowing to Lee, he said gallantly, "An unexpected and very welcome pleasure, ma'am."

"Thank you, Sir Galahad," Lee said.

Ignoring Roman's presence, Hazelhurst asked, "Have you been invited to supper?"

Lee placed a slender finger against her temple as if in deep thought; she looked at Roman and asked, "Have I been asked to supper?"

"Yes," Roman said flatly. "And you accepted."

"Did I?" Lee murmured. "How absentminded of me! Must be my advanced age."

"Well, some other time," Hazelhurst said good-naturedly. Then he looked at Roman and announced, "I'm having a tough enough time keeping the settlers pacified, without you making it worse, Ben."

"So?"

"I don't know what Joe Grimshaw said that caused you to hit him. Perhaps you were justified. But it took me two hours of steady talking to convince him that his damage claim should be postponed." On his way to the door he added, "And I also talked him out of coming after you with a gun."

"Why, that was real nice of you," Roman said with mock admiration. "Be sure to tell Monroe about it so he can write you up in his paper. Land agent saves general manager's life at great risk to himself."

For once Hazelhurst seemed genuinely wrathful. Perhaps it was Lee Farnum's presence, or an accumulation of resentments. "You're a stubborn, stupid fool!" he shouted, his voice high-pitched with emotion. "You're riding for a fall!"

Then he stomped out of the office, and Lee Farnum said softly, "He hates you, Ben."

Roman chuckled. "Should that trouble me?"

"Perhaps. At least you ought to keep it in mind. Clark is awfully ambitious, Ben. He wants your job."

"Well, that's nothing to fight about. Maybe I'll give it to him. Another day like this has been and he's welcome to the damn job."

Lee smiled at him. "You'd rather be at the construction camp, bossing a gang of roughnecks. But this is where you belong."

She got off the desk. She picked up his hat and placed it on his head. "Come look at the warehouse," she invited eagerly. "I'll show you how it can be turned into a hospital."

"But we've got no cash for anything but payrolls and materials," Roman protested.

"That's all this will take, and very little of either," Lee assured him. "Come on, Ben. It won't cost anything to look."

Several people saw them go along the hot street, the lady doctor clinging to Roman's arm and smiling up at him as she talked. Without exception, the watchers waited to see if the couple turned in at Roman's quarters, savoring what seemed to be a spicy story in the making. They were disappointed and somewhat mystified to see Roman and the lady doctor go on to the warehouse.

One of the watchers was Frank Monroe, who presently reported what he had seen to Slim Lacey.

CHAPTER EIGHTEEN

The wind came out of the northwest at dawn. It whipped through San Gorgonia Pass, scooping dust from the dry land and fashioning rippled patterns in the sand dunes south of Salton Sink. By ten o'clock the sun was obscured in a tawny twilight of swirling grit that formed miniature drifts against the closed doors and tent flaps of Deseronto.

Dust sifted between warped boards and window casings, through every crack and cranny. It formed a talcum coating on the dishes Slim Lacey arranged for her noon trade. Her eyes and nostrils were irritated by an abrasive fog that wavered like tan smoke in the lamplit restaurant. But it was the wind that bothered her most: the thin, wild whine hour after hour. There was a loneliness in it, a sense of desolation. Even though the wind was hot, it reminded Slim of winter winds in Iowa that had frightened her as a little girl. On stormy nights the wind had moaned around the gable of her attic bedroom, sounding so scary that she'd covered her head with the quilts.

The continuous patter of sand against the window now was like the sound of blizzard-driven snow, and there was the same monotonous moaning of the wind.

Slim was glad when a customer came in before noon. A hardware drummer turned cranky by the storm, he complained about sand in his soup; but Slim felt better while he was at the counter. The dust-fogged lamplight seemed less weird with someone to share it.

When the drummer departed there was another interval of wind-shrill aloneness before the door opened again and Ben Roman hustled inside.

"What a day!" he said, rubbing grit from his eyes.

"The wind is awful," Slim said. "It makes me so nervous I could scream."

That admission surprised Ben Roman, and somehow pleased him. She was usually so self-sufficient. In all the time he had known Slim, she had never complained about anything before. He asked, "Does the wind bother you that much?"

Slim nodded. "Is there anything odd about that?"

"Why, no," Roman admitted.

"Then why are you gawking at me?"

Roman laughed. He reached across the counter and tweaked her chin. "Big Slim can take heat and dust and flies without a word," he teased, "but wind makes her spooky as an old maid with a mouse in her bustle."

Slim couldn't help smiling as she poured him a cup of coffee. He was like his old self, she thought; like the Ben Roman who had once called her his kind of woman. . . .

"First time you've smiled in a week," Roman said. "I thought you were mad at me."

"I was," she said.

"Why?"

"No use talking about it, Ben."

"Was it because I fired Doc Shumway?"

She nodded.

"So that's it," Roman mused. "What a thing to get mad about!" Then he asked impatiently, "Can't you get it through your head that it was a thing I had to do?"

"Did you?" she asked.

"Of course I had to. I felt sorry for Doc. I didn't like to fire him. But that isn't important. I've got to think of the project, and the great mass of people it will benefit later on."

Slim eyed him wonderingly. "But I thought you didn't give a darn about the settlers," she said. "You told me once that you could like a person, but not people."

Roman shrugged. "Changed my way of thinking."

Slim continued to look at him with a sober attentiveness. She asked, "Did Lee Farnum cause the change?"

"Well, she thinks the same as John Chilton did, and I believe he was right."

Slim shook her head. "You never believed

Chilton was right, Ben. Why, you told me his thinking was loco."

"Well, can't a man change his mind?" Roman demanded. "By God, am I supposed to explain everything I think?"

"Nobody asked you to explain anything," Slim reminded him. "I told you there was no use talking about it."

But now it seemed important for her to understand his side of it; to know why he'd had to discharge Doc Shumway. He said, "Look, Slim. I'm general manager of a project that's bigger than Doc, or Hazelhurst or Frank Monroe. It's bigger than all of them put together. I want to keep the project going until Southern Pacific comes in with us. That's the only chance we've got — to hang on until S.P. comes in."

"But what's that got to do with Doc Shumway?" Slim asked.

Roman scowled at her. "Can't you understand what I've been trying to say?" he demanded.

"All I understand is that you've changed, Ben. And I'm sorry."

"Why?"

"Because I liked Ben Roman the way he was."

"Much?" Roman inquired.

"Too much, I guess. You talked tough, and you acted as if you didn't give a darn for anyone, but there was a kindness in you,

Ben. It was a nice thing."

"And now, because I fired Doc Shumway, you don't like me any more?"

"It's not just that. It's because Lee Farnum has changed you."

As if talking to himself, Roman said, "So Big Slim has a jealous streak in her. She thinks I've got a case on the lady doctor."

"Haven't you?"

Roman shook his head. He fingered the bracelet he had given her. "The man in Tucson said you were the prettiest girl in Deseronto."

"But that was before Lee Farnum came here."

"Don't listen to Frank Monroe," Roman said. "He's a suspicious old woman. A reformer. I had no choice about Doc Shumway. He was drunk when we needed him at the construction camp. Hazelhurst brought Lee Farnum, and I had to give her the job."

Slim thought about that for a moment before saying, "Then it wasn't just to make a place for her."

"Hell, no. I turned her down once. You know that. But when she proved how capable she was, I had to hire her. Lee Farnum is a first-class doctor, Slim. She proved that at Pilot Knob."

"And pretty," Slim mused, giving him a sly smile.

Presently, as she came from behind the

counter and dusted off the stools, Roman asked, "Heard from your dad lately?"

"Last week. He's going to Alaska."

"Wonderful place, Alaska," Roman said. "Joe is a lucky dog."

"A tramp dog," Slim said. "I'll probably never see him again."

Roman put an arm around her shoulder. "Well, like I mentioned before, you've still got me."

Slim shook her head. "The project has you, Ben. I'm just an individual who doesn't count."

"You always counted with me," Roman insisted.

She remained passive and silent within the circle of his arm. A faint smiling softened her lips as he continued to look at her. "You counted with me, too," she said finally. "I guess you know that."

Roman said, "Slim," and brought her to him so abruptly that she dropped the dustcloth. The scent of her hair was like an intimate perfume for him; color stained her cheeks and some flame of emotion glowed in her eyes. She was a warmth and a fragrance in his arms. She was what a man wanted when he wanted a woman.

Slim's hands came against his chest with defensive pressure and her lips slid away. "No, Ben," she protested. "Someone's at the door."

181

She pulled free and went quickly behind the counter as Jim Brimberry came in.

"Why don't you knock?" Roman demanded.

"What for?"

The baffled expression on Brimberry's roan cheeks made Slim laugh. But she felt sorry for him, and said, "Ben is just funning with you, Mohee."

"Storm must've made him loco," Brimberry muttered, and climbed onto a stool. "It's gettin' worse. Regular damn hurricane. I told Miss Farnum she shouldn't go."

"Go where?" Roman demanded.

"To Lateral Seventeen. She's got a case of typhoid fever at the Van Horns'."

Roman stared at him. "You mean to say she started for there in this storm?"

Brimberry nodded.

"You shouldn't have let her go."

"Well, I tried to talk her out of it. I said this was too much of a storm for a lady to be traipsin' around in a buggy. But you know how she is. Knows it all, by God."

"How long ago did she leave?"

"Upwards of half an hour."

As Roman turned away from the counter, Slim asked, "Where you going, Ben?"

"To bring her back, if I can find her," Roman said, and slammed the door behind him.

Slim went to the front window. She

couldn't see Ben, or the building across the street. Everything was hidden by an opaque haze of wind-driven dust.

"Wouldn't you think a growed woman would have more sense than to start out in a sandstorm?" Brimberry grumbled. "And her a danged greenhorn, to boot."

"That's why," Slim said. "She's a greenhorn."

She thought: A blonde, sweet-smiling greenhorn who has her mind set on marrying Ben Roman.

Mohee Jim ordered his meal. When Slim brought it from the kitchen, he said, "I hope Ben thinks to take a canteen with him. He's liable to spend the night in a sand drift. I've seen it so bad out on them flats that a man couldn't tell up from down, to say nothin' of north and south."

The risk to Ben hadn't occurred to Slim. Now it did, and she said urgently, "Go with him, Mohee. Or if he's already gone, fill a canteen and follow him. It wouldn't be so risky with two, if you've got water."

"But I'm hungry," Mohee objected. "You can't expect a man to leave his vittles —"

Slim grasped his arm. "You've got to go," she insisted, and propelled him toward the door.

As he went out she called after him, "Don't forget the canteen."

CHAPTER NINETEEN

It took Ben Roman about three minutes to saddle his bay gelding, and another couple of minutes to fill a canteen. The wind was at his back as he left town, but the billowing grit half blinded him. He peered at the dust-swirled road, finding no sign of travel until he came to a sand drift and glimpsed two fragile ruts.

"The darned fool," he muttered.

But Roman understood why Lee Farnum wouldn't let a sandstorm interfere with her duty as a doctor. She had to prove that a woman doctor was capable; that she could cope with anything the job involved. Proud, he thought; proud and stubborn, and ambitious. She had wanted this job, and she'd got it. She wanted a hospital and she was getting that. Roman smiled, thinking how adroitly she had drawn Deseronto's leading citizens into her hospital project. Oscar Hoffman was donating ten beds and mattresses, and she had talked Lew Gallatin into contributing a hundred dollars toward the general fund, which was already nearing the thousand-dollar mark.

A natural-born organizer, Roman thought.

Recalling Slim's accusation that Lee had changed him, he understood that she had altered his attitude toward the project. Not changed it, exactly, but made his job as general manager seem more important, more worth while. Not that he cared much what happened after Southern Pacific came in, if it did. John Chilton had asked him to stay with it that long, and he would, unless Imperial went broke first.

Alternately loping and trotting, Roman rode through successive drifts that were almost knee-deep to the bay. When he came to a storm-shrouded shack at the forks of the road he stopped long enough to learn that Lee had taken the south fork, and that she was about fifteen minutes ahead of him.

"We tried to talk her into putting up with us until the wind went down," the settler reported. "But she had her mind set on reachin' the Van Horn place."

His wife, busy at the stove, said, "We're having side meat and hominy grits for supper. You're welcome to stay and eat."

"Why, that's mighty kind of you," Roman said. "I can't spare the time now, but next time I'm by this way I'd sure like to accept your invitation."

The woman, who was heavy with child, shook her head. "We might be gone from here by then," she said in a flat, resigned voice.

And one of the three youngsters announced, "We're goin' back to Tennessee."

Roman opened the door and motioned for the settler to step outside with him. Presently, standing in the lee of the shed's east wall, Roman asked, "You need money for the trip?"

"Well, we ain't got any to speak of," the man admitted. "But I ain't down to charity yet."

"How about a loan?" Roman suggested.

The man shook his head. "At the rate my woman is producin' babies, I wouldn't ever be able to pay off a loan. What I need worst is a steady job at day's wages."

"Then you've got one," Roman said. "Soon as the wind dies down, go to Pilot Knob and tell Moynihan I sent you."

A pleased smile altered the man's gaunt face. "You mean a steady job — not just temporary?"

"For as long as you want," Roman said, and climbed into the saddle.

Riding away from the wind-whipped shack, he liked his job for the first time. Perhaps individuals weren't important, but the smile on that man's face seemed so.

Afterward, as he rode south, the wind was worse. Its shrill voice was like a sustained scream and its pelting pressure caused the bay to veer constantly to the left. The thought came to Roman that Lee's horse might also drift off the road, without her noticing it. There were no fences here, no visible landmarks.

A tumbleweed, bouncing across the road like a huge rubber ball, spooked Roman's horse. When they passed a greasewood thicket the wind came through in a two-toned, reedy whistle. Some time after that Roman glimpsed a shack just west of the road, and was surprised that he had come this far. Elliott's place, he thought; but presently, as he knocked and the door opened, Roman understood that he had passed Elliott's house without seeing it. This man who scowled at him from the doorway was Joe Grimshaw.

"Did you see a buggy go by?" Roman asked.

Grimshaw nodded.

"How long ago?"

"None of your goddamn business," Grimshaw snapped, and slammed the door.

"To hell with you!" Roman shouted. But he felt better, knowing that Lee had got this far. She was still on the road, at least.

The next drift seemed longer and deeper than any he had encountered. Roman observed wheel marks at the north end of it, and presently glimpsed a trampled place where the horse had bogged down before going on.

The bay lunged through deep sand for

what seemed half a mile before the drift leveled off. Roman searched for wheel marks, and found none; he rode back across the drift, scanning wind-rippled sand. There were no tracks, except the bay's, and those were filling fast.

Worried now, Roman gave his horse a brief rest while he considered the next move. Lee had started through this drift, but seemingly hadn't reached the south end of it. Had she been forced to turn back, and passed him unseen in the billowing dust? Or had her horse angled off to the easement of the road?

Roman took a swig from the canteen. It occurred to him that he hadn't asked Grimshaw which direction the buggy was traveling when it passed his shack. He could go back and force the disgruntled settler to tell him. But that would take time, and there wasn't much daylight left. Roman decided to circle eastward. If he was to find Lee, it would have to be soon.

Roman was rimming the north edge of the drift when a bullet went past his cheek, that metallic *whang* of sound instantly followed by a gun blast behind him. Glancing back, Roman glimpsed an obscure shape in the tawny haze. He thought: Grimshaw, and spurred the bay into a lunging run.

Two more bullets slashed close to Roman as he roweled his horse in zigzag flight. He thought: The dirty son is trying to kill me, and the shock of that realization made his shoulder muscles crawl. Clark Hazelhurst hadn't made up the story about Grimshaw's threat to come after him with a gun. The big Kansan was on the warpath for sure!

Abruptly then, as a buggy top loomed ahead of him, Roman jerked the bay into a sharp right turn. He was remotely aware of Lee Farnum's excited voice behind him. He heard the blast of Grimshaw's gun, and, looking back, saw that the settler had changed course with him.

There was another shot, the report muffled by the wind's howling, and then two more reports that were barely audible. Roman knew then that he was outrunning Grimshaw. He changed course again and looked back, seeing no sign of movement in the dust-clotted gloom. But Grimshaw, he realized, might be within fifty feet of him. The visibility was that bad.

Roman gave his panting horse a breather. Peering into the swirling haze, he observed movement off to the left. He tightened his reins, ready to wheel the bay around, then relaxed as a tumbleweed went bouncing past. He waited out another five minutes of patient watchfulness, not sure whether Grimshaw was ahead of him now, or behind him. The buggy, Roman calculated, was about due north of him and not more than a mile away. He wondered if it was stuck in a drift, and hoped it was; otherwise Lee might wander farther from the road and be harder to find.

Roman cursed the dust that irritated his eyes and nostrils. He uncorked the canteen, took a drink, and used a wet finger to wash out his eyes. This, he reflected, was what happened when a woman tried to do a man's work. Why couldn't women be satisfied to act like women? You wouldn't catch Slim Lacey sashaying around in a sandstorm. She stayed in the house, where a woman belonged.

Remembering his reaction the day of Lee Farnum's arrival in Deseronto, Roman thought: I was right, and should've stuck to it. This damned desert was no place for a lady doctor.

But presently, as he rode northward and saw no sign of Grimshaw, Roman's mood changed. Lee shouldn't be blamed for going to a patient in a sandstorm; even though it was a hazardous, foolhardy thing, she deserved some credit for attempting it.

He set a northward course by keeping his left cheek to the wind. When he had covered what he believed was a mile, it occurred to Roman that the wind might have changed direction enough to throw him off. It was almost dark now. "Won't see the rig until I'm on top of it," he muttered.

Warily watchful for sign of movement,

Roman wondered if Grimshaw were still on the prowl. The Kansan might have given up and gone home. But there was no telling what a loco sodbuster would do. Grimshaw might flounder around in the storm all night hoping to bump into a target.

Convinced that he had come far enough north, Roman turned eastward, intending to circle. He had ridden a dozen paces when the remote sound of gunfire came to him — three shots in succession. Pulling up, Roman listened. For a long moment there was only the monotonous rushing of the wind. Then it came again, three spaced reports.

"A signal," he muttered.

But why should Grimshaw be signaling?

It occurred to Roman that Lee might have a pistol; that she might be firing to attract aid. Curious and suspicious, Roman turned the bay westward. Presently the triple reports came again, louder now and to the right. Roman took out his pocket knife. If this was Grimshaw, there might be a chance to use it at close quarters.

When Roman glimpsed the buggy's vague shape he was within ten feet of it. In the same moment Mohee Jim loomed up beside it and called, "Light down, Ben."

"What you doing here?" Roman demanded.

"Well, I took out after you, and ran into Joe Grimshaw," Brimberry explained. "He throwed a shot at me, and I throwed one back at him." Mohee Jim chuckled. "Mine winged him."

"Where is he?" Roman asked, dismounting.

Mohee Jim gestured toward the buggy. "Havin' his arm fixed by the lady doctor."

"How'd you find her?" Roman demanded.

"Grimshaw seen the buggy while he was chasin' you," Mohee Jim said. "He was scairt loony, thinkin' he might bleed to death. Couldn't get here fast enough."

"So the lady doctor gets found by three men," Roman mused, leading his horse toward the buggy. "She's a regular damn magnet for attracting stray males."

A moment later Lee Farnum asked urgently, "Are you all right, Ben?"

"Good as can be expected in such weather," he said, and had his look at Grimshaw.

The settler's face was tight with pain. He grunted as Lee tied a bandage around his right arm above the elbow and asked in a whining voice, "You sure the bone ain't broke?"

Lee shook her head, and as Grimshaw got out of the buggy, Roman said, "Maybe I'll break it, Grimshaw. Maybe I'll break every bone in your body."

The settler shrank back against the buggy, holding up his left palm in a defensive gesture. "I wasn't tryin' to hit you," he said.

"Like hell you weren't!"

Grimshaw shook his head. "Just tried to spook you is all. On account of that beatin' you gave me. Honest, Roman, that's all I was doin'."

Watching from the buggy, Lee Farnum saw rage-prodded savagery alter Ben Roman's face. He said, "You stinking liar," and hit Grimshaw in the face.

The big Kansan yelped and went to his knees. "I ain't lyin'!" he whispered. "Honest I ain't."

Roman turned to Mohee Jim, who was holding two horses. He said, "Get him out of here before I stomp him to death."

Afterward, driving the rig toward the road while Mohee Jim led the bay gelding, Roman asked, "Did you know you were lost, Lee?"

She nodded and gripped his arm tighter. "I was terribly frightened, Ben. So frightened I prayed."

"For a compass?"

Lee shook her head. She tipped her face against his shoulder and said, "For you to come and find me."

Roman got an arm around her. It was full dark now and he couldn't see her face, but he knew she was smiling.

"Reward?" he asked, and was pleased by the eager response of her lips.

She wasn't thinking about a hospital now. But she was aroused.

CHAPTER TWENTY

The wind was still blowing when Mohee Jim Brimberry came into Lacey's Restaurant a little after nine o'clock. Slim sat at the counter with Frank Monroe, a checkerboard between them. As Brimberry came to the counter, Monroe made a double jump, taking two of her men.

"What's the matter with you tonight?" Frank inquired.

Slim shrugged. "Must be the wind."

Going behind the counter, she poured a cup of coffee for Mohee Jim and asked, "Did you catch up with Ben?"

Brimberry nodded. He said wearily, "What a day to be polishin' a saddle, and with no vittles since breakfast!"

"How about a T-bone steak?" Slim suggested.

Brimberry nodded. "Two of 'em, and a double ration of potatoes."

When Slim went to the kitchen, Frank Monroe asked, "Where you been, Mohee?"

"Yonderly. Way to hell and gone yonderly."

"With Ben Roman?"

"Part of the time."

"What were you doing?"

194

"Ridin', mostly."

Monroe peered at Brimberry, baffled by this seeming reticence from a man who was usually so free with his talk. What, he wondered, could be the reason for Mohee's odd behavior? Endeavoring to mask an increasing curiosity, Monroe asked casually, "A secret deal?"

"Well, sort of. Ben said not to mention it to nobody." Mohee chuckled. "It'd sure make a story for your newspaper, though. A heller of a story."

Slim called from the kitchen, "You want them rare, Mohee?"

"The first one. I'm that hungry I could almost eat it raw."

Monroe got out a brier pipe and tamped tobacco into it. Here, he felt sure, was a proposition worthy of his reportorial skill; a good story that he'd have to dig for. "Is Ben at his quarters?" he asked, deciding on an oblique approach.

Mohee Jim shook his head.

"Any idea when he will be?"

Brimberry gave the question a little thought. "Don't reckon he'll get back until way after midnight."

Monroe couldn't understand it. He asked, "Can't you even tell me where Ben is?"

"Sure," Mohee Jim said. "There's no secret about that." The appetizing odor of frying steak assailed his nostrils now and he said, "I guess there ain't no nicer thing in this whole

195

damned world to smell than sizzlin' beef when you're hungry. Don't that make your mouth water, Frank?"

"No," Monroe muttered. "I've had supper."

Brimberry peered at him. "Ain't you ever missed any meals, Frank?"

Monroe shook his head. "Where is Ben?" he asked impatiently.

"At the Van Horns', or should be by now."

Monroe thought about that for a moment. "That's where Dr. Farnum went. Did Ben go with her?"

"You mean to the Van Horns'?"

Monroe nodded, irritated by the slow progress he was making, yet confident that he would get the story eventually.

"Well, if she got there, he did. Leastwise, he was with Miss Farnum last I saw of her."

"When was that?"

"Sometime after dark. Don't know exactly what time of day it was."

"Where?"

"Well, I ain't exactly sure about that either. Hard to see landmarks at night with a sandstorm blowin'. But it was betwixt Grimshaw's place and the Van Horns'."

Exasperated now, and wholly confused, Monroe demanded, "Why should there be anything secret about Ben Roman accompanying Miss Farnum to call on a patient during a sandstorm?"

"There ain't."

196

"But I thought you said Ben didn't want you to tell me about it."

"Oh, he didn't mean that," Brimberry said. "It's the other part he don't want told."

"What other part?"

"Why, the part I ain't tellin' you," Mohee Jim said, chuckling.

When Slim brought in the first steak he smacked his lips and exclaimed, "Food, by God! Food for the starving!"

CHAPTER TWENTY-ONE

It was still storming when Ben Roman returned from Lateral 17 at noon of the second day. George Frayne reported that the railroad telegraph wires were down, and four freight trains were marooned just east of Deseronto by drifting sand.

"The crews walked back and are eating at Slim Lacey's," he said. "She's doing a big business."

Soon after that a wild-eyed young settler came in asking for Dr. Farnum. "My wife was having bad labor pains when I left," Lloyd Tatum announced. "This is her first baby."

"Dr. Farnum is at the Van Horns'," Roman said.

"Way out there? Then I'll have to ask Doc Shumway." Tatum grimaced, adding, "I sure hate to, though. My wife quit him soon as she heard there was a lady doctor. Marybelle figured it would be less embarrassing when her time came. But I'll have to ask him, regardless."

"Shumway is at Karen Borgstrom's," Roman said. "Her boy is sick."

Tatum stared at him with wide, startled

eyes. "Then what'll I do?" he asked, his voice high-pitched with alarm. "This is Marybelle's first baby and she's awful scared."

No worse scared than you, Roman thought. He asked, "Is your place nearer to Mrs. Borgstrom's than to the Van Horns'?"

Tatum nodded. He stood there as if dazed beyond the power of speech or movement.

"Then why don't you go get Doc Shumway?" Roman suggested.

"You reckon he'd come, being on a case, and my wife quitting him like she did?"

Roman nodded. "Tell Doc I sent you. Tell him I said it would be a favor to me."

"Much obliged," Tatum said, and hurried out into the dust-hazed street.

The sandstorm continued for another day and another night, then ceased abruptly. After four days of howling wind, the calm seemed odd and the dustless clarity of this fifth morning revealed a string of boxcars extending eastward as far as the eye could see. It was noon before the trains began moving, and after sundown when the last caboose rumbled past the Southern Pacific depot.

Ben Roman had finished supper and was having his third cup of coffee at Slim's counter when Lee Farnum came into the restaurant. "So the wanderer returns," he said. "How's the Van Horn boy?"

"Out of danger, I think," Lee said. "But he had a bad time."

She took the stool beside Roman. She smiled at Slim and asked, "What's good for supper?"

"All I have left is beef stew," Slim said. "The railroaders ate up everything else."

"Then beef stew it is," Lee agreed.

Turning to Roman, she ceased smiling. A weariness showed in her face as she said, "I stopped by the Tatum place and found day-old twins."

"Twins," Roman echoed. "Young Tatum must be mighty proud of himself."

"He said you suggested he get Dr. Shumway. Is that so, Ben?"

Roman nodded. Strongly aware of her calculating appraisal, he said, "Didn't like the idea of you busting out into that storm again."

She eyed him intently, her face grave. "Was that the only reason?"

"Well, not exactly."

"Then what was it?"

Roman shrugged. Resenting her inquisitiveness, he said, "What difference does it make? Tatum's wife needed a doctor. She got one, and her husband got twins. Isn't that enough?"

"I want to know, Ben."

Roman took out his Durham sack and gave his attention to shaping a cigarette. This, he thought, was what you could expect from a woman working a man's job. She wasn't satisfied to leave well enough alone.

"Was it because you believed it would make Dr. Shumway feel good, thinking he was needed?" she asked.

Roman nodded. Bracing himself for an argument, he said, "That's it exactly," and was astonished at the swift change in her face. She had appeared angry, or on the verge of anger. Now she smiled and said, "I'm glad you did it."

As Slim brought her supper, Lee added, "But if it had been to keep me out of the storm, I would have resigned."

Roman laughed at her. "I can see you resigning," he scoffed. "Why, they couldn't drive you away from here with a club."

"I mean it, Ben. I insist on working the job as a doctor, not as a woman."

Presently she said, "I stopped by at the Borgstrom place, too."

"How's Karen's boy?"

"Still quite sick. But Dr. Shumway will save him." She smiled, adding, "The boy probably doesn't know it, but he's going to have a stepfather. The wedding date is set. They'll be married when the circuit-riding minister comes through in September."

"If Doc stops drinking that long?"

Lee shook her head. "Karen says the drinking makes no difference. She thinks Doc won't want whisky when he has a wife."

"Well, she might be able to keep him sober

most of the time," Roman said, "but she'll never turn him into a farmer."

"That shouldn't be necessary, Ben. I told Dr. Shumway there were more patients than one doctor could take proper care of."

"So?"

"I said I was going to request that you put him on the payroll."

Roman peered at her. "You mean two doctors?"

Lee nodded. "It's ridiculous for so large a project to have only one doctor." Turning to Slim, she asked, "Don't you agree?"

Slim thought about it for a moment, regarding Lee with a grave intentness.

Watching these two young women face each other across the counter, Roman observed how unlike they were. It was more than the difference between blonde and brunette, or between a restaurant keeper and a lady doctor. It went deeper than that; an inherent, basic difference that influenced their thinking.

"Running the new hospital will probably take up most of your time," Slim said finally.

"But that has nothing to do with it," Lee insisted. "This is a growing community of far-spaced homes. Just because people got along with one doctor is no reason why they should always have to do it." She made an impatient gesture. Directing her talk to

Roman now, she said, "I know what you're thinking. When the company had a man doctor, one was enough. But that's wrong, Ben. One wasn't enough. Folks just went without medical attention, week after week. For months, sometimes, until what ailed them became chronic. And that's not right."

"They're poor folks, and the company is poor too," Roman said. "We thought we were living high off the hog when we got our first doctor. Until then there wasn't one nearer than Yuma."

Lee said, "You're still thinking of this as an uninhabited desert. It hasn't occurred to you that new babies are arriving all the time, and that the number of births will probably double next year. This is a growing community, Ben — a place where young couples are raising families and the population will increase all the time."

Roman asked with mock suspicion, "You been keeping company with Clark Hazelhurst?"

"No, but I'm sure he would agree that we need two doctors. With Shumway taking over most of the practice out there, I could handle the hospital and be available when needed at the construction camp. It would work out so well, Ben, and it's so necessary."

Roman winked at Slim. "She missed her calling. Should've been a real-estate promoter."

"But don't you see how much better it would be?" Lee asked.

Roman nodded. He said with exaggerated reluctance, "You win, if I can put it over with the Los Angeles office."

A newspaper boy opened the screen door and announced, "Weekly Clarion!"

Roman bought three, giving Slim and Lee each a newspaper before scanning the front page. There was a brief item about the settlers' claims, and the fact that Imperial's general manager had "fist-whipped Joe Grimshaw out of the office."

Roman smiled. He thought: If Monroe only knew the rest of that story! Finding no mention of Gallatin's saloon deal, he read the featured piece:

GOVERNMENT TRIES NEW TRICK TO RUIN IMPERIAL VALLEY

The Reclamation Service is attempting a new maneuver that, if successful, will ruin the Imperial Development project. According to a Washington press release, Reclamation Chief F. H. Newell contends that the Colorado River is a navigable stream and therefore the company's diversion is illegal. His announcement is so phrased as to imply that Imperial Development has been the tool of greedy villains perpetuating a hoax. We who have known such men as John Chilton, Ronald Florsheim, and Clark Hazelhurst know that they have been dedicated to the welfare of the Valley; that they are neither greedy nor crooked.

This latest attack by Theodore Roosevelt's reclamation pets is in line with Milton Whitney's ill-famed publication of the Agriculture Department survey announcing that most of the Valley's soil was so impregnated with alkali that all possibility of agriculture was precluded. It was that grossly erroneous report that ruined the company's financial standing in Eastern banking circles and brought Imperial Development to near bankruptcy.

It is hoped that this new and dastardly attack will be recognized for what it is — the senseless braying of thumb-twiddling bureaucrats!

"Roosevelt and his rough-riding politicians," Roman muttered.

Lee asked, "Why wasn't your name included with Chilton's, Florsheim's, and Hazelhurst's?"

Roman grinned. "Because I'm not dedicated."

"But you are," Lee said. "You've got the good of the Valley at heart."

Roman shook his head. "As a matter of fact, I don't give a damn about it, Lee. Just want to lick the river, is all."

Mohee Jim opened the screen door and announced, "You're wanted at the hotel, Miss Farnum. A man with a busted head."

Roman went to the doorway with her. He asked, "What happened, Mohee?"

"Tony Caruso brought him in. Tony says there was a free-for-all fight and this jigger got hit over the head with a bottle. Damned near scalped him."

Afterward, while Lee Farnum took care of the injured man, Caruso told Roman about the fight. "It's that new saloon Gallatin opened up. The men drink for four days and do no work."

"So that's it," Roman muttered. Remembering that Gallatin had been in town during the storm, he asked, "Who's running the saloon?"

"Black Mike Moynihan. He quit his job and went into partnership with Gallatin."

"The big Irish dunce!" Roman exclaimed. Then he demanded, "Why wasn't I told about this before?"

"The storm," Caruso explained. "Mr. MacIvor said you should be told, but there was too much storm."

CHAPTER TWENTY-TWO

Black Mike Moynihan was a trifle drunk and happy as a man could be. For the first time in his life he stood on the money side of a bar. Fifty cents of every dollar that crossed the crude counter was his. In five days as a saloonkeeper he had made more than a gang foreman got for a month of hard work. Of course, the sandstorm had helped trade considerably. Mike chuckled, recalling how eagerly the camp's idle workers had patronized his bar. And except for one big fight, there'd been no trouble at all.

Dispensing drinks with a fine flourish, Moynihan beamed at his customers. " 'Twas a grand and glorious day for us all when Lew Gallatin opened this saloon," he told them. "What good is it to work if a man can't belly up to a bar of an evenin'?"

When a bleary-eyed laborer discovered that his pockets were devoid of cash, Moynihan said, "Think nothin' about it, Martin. Nothin' at all. Ye can settle with me on payday." Pouring the man his drink, Mike added softly, "But be goddamn sure ye do so."

"I won't forget," the man said.

"That ye will not," Mike promised. "I'll see

to it that ye don't forget."

Moynihan hummed a cheery tune. It lacked half an hour of midnight and there were upwards of twenty men in the smoke-hazed tent. Most of them still had money to spend. A man could get rich at this business; he could wear stylish clothes and buy himself a diamond ring and have a fancy woman to keep him company.

Me luck has changed at last, he told himself. Now I'm goin' to make a fortune.

He was polishing a glass when Ben Roman and Mohee Jim entered the tent. "Come have a drink on the house," he invited them graciously, and as they came up to the bar, he asked, "What'll ye have, gints? Bourbon or rye?"

"Neither," Roman said. "We're closing this place."

"Closin' it?" Moynihan asked, his smile fading. "Ye mean a twelve-o'clock curfew?"

Roman shook his head. "I mean you're going out of the saloon business, Mike."

Moynihan peered at him in bug-eyed wonderment. "Ye must be funnin' me," he said.

"I'll not have a saloon in this camp," Roman announced. Watching Moynihan's expression change from disbelief to anger, he said, "Lew Gallatin jobbed you, Mike. He knew there'd be trouble, and he wanted you to take it."

"Trouble, me eye!" Moynihan scoffed, and

glanced at the men who lined his bar. "These boys want a place to take a sociable nip of an evenin'. Where's the trouble in that?"

One of the customers shouted, "You're right, Moynihan. Absolutely right!"

And another called, "Don't let him hooraw you, Mike."

"Ye hear?" Moynihan asked. "Ye'll not close this place, Ben Roman. I'm surprised that ye'd even think of it, and ye a man I cared for like a brother — a man who'd stand up to Michael Moynihan with his fists. I'm ashamed of ye, Ben Roman. Ashamed and mortified."

"Are you going to close up, or do we close you?" Roman asked flatly.

"Ye'll not close this place, Ben Roman. 'Tis a business establishmint that doesn't concern ye at all."

Roman turned to Brimberry and said, "Go get a can of kerosene."

As Mohee Jim went out, Moynihan came from behind the plank bar. "I'll take no more lip from ye," he warned. "Git out, or I'll throw ye out."

Roman shouldered a drunken man aside, making room for himself with his back to the bar. He said, "No need to have trouble, Mike. You can go on the job as foreman tomorrow morning."

Moynihan loosed a hoot of derisive laughter. "Ah, I can, can I?" he cried, his voice shrill with outrage. "Me, that's become the proprietor of a fine saloon!"

He came up in front of Roman and shook a huge fist at him and said again, "Git out!"

Roman was strongly aware of attentive faces forming a close-ranked ring behind Moynihan. Eager, expectant faces. This smoke-fouled tent had been noisy with talk and laughter a few moments ago; now a strict silence prevailed. Roman recalled the fight on the train and wondered if he could whip this big Irishman again, and had his doubts. He'd have to hit him first — and hard.

"Are ye deef?" Moynihan demanded. "I said git out!"

Roman glanced toward the doorway. Mohee Jim might not show for another five or ten minutes, which was longer than this rage-prodded Irishman would wait. So thinking, Roman peered past Moynihan and called, "Douse the canvas with kerosene!"

As Moynihan turned to look, Roman hit him on the jaw with a sledging right that jarred the big Irishman into a tilted, dance-like shuffle. He rocked Moynihan with successive lefts and rights to the face and stepped back as Mike took a wild swing at him. The margin of that miss told Roman something: Those first blows had befuddled Black Mike. Roman blocked a two-fisted attack with his guarding arms and slugged

Moynihan in the belly.

Black Mike squawked a curse. He backed off and wiped his bleeding nose on an uphunched shoulder. "I'll smash ye to smithereens!" he shouted, and lunged at Roman again.

The lust for battle was a bright shine in Moynihan's eyes, but there was an odd deliberateness in the way he handled his fists. It was as if he took time to think between each swing. Roman avoided his clumsy charge by weaving aside. Moynihan endeavored to check, but his fist smashed against the plank bar. He yelped and wheeled around, looking for Roman. He sucked his bruised knuckles and panted, "Why don't ye stand and fight?"

Roman waited, wanting to end this with one well-placed blow. He wasn't aware of Angus MacIvor's presence in the crowd until Angus urged, "Finish him off, Ben."

Some friend of Moynihan's snarled, "You keep out of it!"

And now, as Black Mike charged again, Roman heard men scuffling behind him, and understood that a second fight was starting. He dodged away from Moynihan's clubbing fists, pivoted in a complete circle, and clouted Moynihan in the face. The other fight was in full swing now. Roman heard the impact of fists against flesh. He thought: Angus is in it, and was remotely amused by that.

There was something oddly pleasing about this deal. He hit Black Mike and took a blow to the shoulder that spun him against the bar. There was no sensation of pain when Moynihan's fist struck him; just a thrusting urge to strike back, an exultant awareness of muscles and movement. This, he thought, was better than sitting at a desk and listening to complaints. It was a thing a man could work up an honest sweat at, and take some pride in doing.

Roman targeted Moynihan's scowling face with a lancing right and took a punch in the chest that knocked him down. He bounded up instantly. He swung at Moynihan's jaw and missed and was jolted off balance by a man behind him. Crouching as he dodged, Roman heard Moynihan and another man collide, and was grabbed around the neck by a burly laborer who cried, "Here he is, Mike!"

Roman drove a knee into the man's crotch. He rammed his way toward MacIvor and heard Brimberry call, "Ben, where you at?"

"Shoot out the light!" Roman shouted.

Moynihan came at him, bellowing, "Stand, ye spalpeen — stand and fight!"

Roman ripped free of hands that grasped him from behind. He dodged a flung bottle and was slugging it out with Moynihan when Brimberry's gun exploded. There was a crash of cascading glass as the lamplight faded, and now Moynihan howled, "Somebody go git a lantern!"

The dark tent was alive with sound and movement, with raw-voiced cursing and grunting and the thud of fists. Roman grinned. Moynihan's customers were now battling one another. He thought: They don't care who they fight, just so they're fighting. There'd be many a black eye in camp to-morrow.

Roman fought his way toward the entrance and wondered how Angus had fared. A fist smashed his ribs. He struck out wildly and collided with a pair of panting men locked in fierce wrestling. He heard them go down, one man loosing an agonized grunt.

Aware of fresh air cutting through the stench of spilled kerosene and whisky-tainted breath, Roman understood that he was near the doorway. A man bumped into him, de-manded, "Who be you?" and struck without waiting for an answer. Roman crouched, taking the blow across a shoulder. Butting the men aside, he heard Mohee Jim call, "Where are you, Ben?"

Roman turned to the left and glimpsed two vague shapes against the doorway's lesser darkness. He asked, "Is that Angus with you, Mohee?"

"In person," MacIvor muttered, and as Roman moved up to them he said disgust-edly, "What a pack of idiots! Are they going to fight all night?"

Roman asked, "You got the kerosene, Mohee?"

"Better'n three gallons. Where you want it used?"

"On the bar," Roman said. "Go around back and cut a hole in the canvas. Douse the bar and light it, then douse the back wall too."

"How about them kegs behind the bar? Hadn't we better roll them out so's they won't burn up?"

"To hell with Gallatin's booze," Roman said. "I warned him not to open a saloon here."

As Brimberry disappeared into the darkness, Roman said amusedly, "That should end the free-for-all, Angus."

It did.

As the kerosene-drenched bar burst into flame, a man yelled, "Fire!" Then the rear wall of the tent blazed up and terrified men stampeded toward the doorway.

Roman, MacIvor, and Brimberry were having coffee in the cook shack when Black Mike Moynihan came in. The faces of Roman and MacIvor bore marks of battle, but those bruises were superficial compared with the damage that had been done to Black Mike's blood-crusted countenance. One eye was swollen completely shut, strips of hide had been peeled from both cheeks, and blood dribbled from the corners of his cut lips.

Peering at the cook with his good eye, Moynihan said sourly, "I want a bucket of hot water and some salt."

Then he looked at Roman and asked, "Do I run a gang on this stinkin' outfit, or don't I?"

"Sure," Roman said, and smiled at him. "Come have yourself a cup of coffee, Mike."

Diversion from the new cut sent water into the laterals the first week of September. It brought hope to settlers whose fields had escaped the flood, and Frank Monroe heralded the event with a front-page story headlined: "Hazelhurst Plan Saves Crops!"

Ben Roman spent most of his time at the construction camp. During a brief stay in town he sent off a letter to Phil Judson asking what progress he was making with Epes Randolph, and received a one-line note in reply: "Nothing definite yet."

Discussing this with MacIvor, Roman complained, "What are they waiting for, Angus — next year's flood season?"

"Southern Pacific will never put money into this ragtag concern," MacIvor said. "They've got better sense."

Later in the month Doc Shumway and Karen Borgstrom were married by a circuit-riding minister. Settlers from the far-off flats came to town for the wedding and put on a shivaree at the Pioneer Hotel where Doc and Karen spent their wedding night. Swede Erickson got drunk soon after the ceremony, discarding a lifetime rule of moderation. "Why," he demanded of Lew Gallatin, "would she marry a drunken doctor?" The saloonkeeper had no reasonable explanation, nor did French Nellie when Swede discussed it with her later that night.

The following week Lee Farnum opened her new hospital. Oscar Hoffman, speaker for the occasion, announced that the citizens' committee would share the cost of maintaining it, dollar for dollar, with the company. Hoffman spoke eloquently of Deseronto's civic pride, and requested three cheers "for our lovely lady doctor."

Lee Farnum was radiant, as Roman had known she would be. Revealing more emotion than he had ever observed in her, she was like a bride at a wedding.

Slim Lacey noticed this also, for she said to Roman, "I've never seen her so happy, or so beautiful."

"That's what being in love does to a woman," he said.

Slim met his gaze directly. She asked, "Is that it, Ben?"

Roman nodded, and now, as they joined

the crowd going to see the ward, he explained, "She's in love with this tin-roofed warehouse that's been turned into a hospital."

CHAPTER TWENTY-THREE

October was a good month in the Valley. As daytime heat diminished and nights turned cool, men sniffed the smoky pungence of autumn air; they scooped up dirt and let it trickle through their callused fingers. "Such good soil," they said, and their wives remarked about Thanksgiving being near at hand.

When Roman received a report of heavy rains in the north, he conferred with MacIvor, who said confidently, "There'll be no flood this late in the season."

But Roman was uneasy. The cut, now extending beyond both ends of the dynamite dam, was in its most vulnerable stage. Peering at the pile-supported barricade, he understood how inadequate it would be if the Red Bull went on a rampage.

Three days later Mohee Jim rode in with another report. The rains had caused a rise in Gunnison River.

"Too far away to affect us much down here," MacIvor said, and Roman wondered why that prediction sounded familiar to him.

Mohee Jim climbed into the saddle. He said, "They're circulatin' petitions for

Hazelhurst to take your place as general manager of this outfit."

"Who's circulating them?" Roman demanded.

"Well, Joe Grimshaw is takin' one around to all the settlers, askin' them to sign it. The other one is at Gallatin's bar." Mohee Jim chuckled, adding, "Lew sure looked surprised when I signed it."

"You signed it?"

Brimberry nodded. "And I'm hopin' Hazelhurst takes your place."

"So that's it," Roman muttered. "Anything to get me into the Mogollones."

"Sure, Ben. It'd be the biggest favor they ever done you. Even with the weather coolin' off, this ain't no fit place for fellers like us. It's gettin' too damn crowded — too much hustle and bustle. We need a country where there's room enough and time enough."

"But how about women?" Roman asked, very sober about this. "Where would I find another pair like Slim Lacey and the lady doctor?"

Brimberry spat. "You keep fussin' around them and you'll end up married sure as hell," he warned.

"To both of them?"

"Why, no, you idjit. Ain't bein' hitched to one female bad enough?"

Roman shrugged. "Suppose it depends on the female."

"Now, that's a damn-fool notion," Brimberry muttered, and rode off in the slumped, loose-jointed fashion of a man who had spent most of his life asaddle.

Clark Hazelhurst came to Pilot Knob the next afternoon. He called Roman from the engineer's shack and said, "I want you to know that those petitions are none of my doing, Ben. In fact, I've said publicly they shouldn't be circulated."

"And what have you been saying privately?" Roman inquired.

"The same thing, of course. Just because we don't see eye to eye on everything is no indication I want you fired. You believe that, don't you, Ben?"

"I don't give a damn," Roman said, and went back into the engineer's shack.

Angus MacIvor asked, "What's our nosy land agent up to now?"

"Nothing important," Roman muttered. He studied the blueprint on the drawing board. "Will this take more stress than the old one, Angus?"

MacIvor nodded. "It's the stoutest wooden gate that can be built. But I suppose we're wasting our time on it. Nothing less than concrete will stand against summer floods."

They were on their way to supper when Mohee Jim rode in with a report that told of continuing rains extending from the upper basin as far south as Arizona and eastward into New Mexico. Roman handed the report to MacIvor. "The whole damn watershed," he muttered. "I think we're in for trouble, Angus."

"I can't believe it," MacIvor protested, obstinate as always when his scientific deductions were involved. "There hasn't been high water this late in twenty-seven years."

"Well, this may be the exception that proves the rule," Roman said. "The exception that will put us out of business."

After supper, as Brimberry made ready to leave, Roman revealed his apprehension by saying, "You keep in close touch with the telegraph operator, Mohee. If there's mention of a rise in the Bill Williams or the Gila, you come running."

Brimberry didn't return that night or the next morning. At noon Roman saddled his bay gelding and said to MacIvor, "There's probably nothing wrong, but I want to be close to the telegraph office, just in case."

When he got to town Roman learned there was a break in the telegraph line west of Yuma. "Freight train jumped the tracks and knocked down half a mile of poles," the operator told him. "May be evening before they get a line set up."

Walking through the alley that led to Main Street, Roman spoke to Swede Erickson, who was repairing a metal brace on a settler's wagon. The blacksmith winked at the settler.

He said to Roman, "What's this I hear about Clark Hazelhurst taking your job?"

"He's welcome to it," Roman said, and going on, heard the settler say, "If it wasn't for Clark, we'd still be waiting for water."

The great land agent, Roman thought disgustedly. Hazelhurst, who had a talent for getting on the right side of people, was a hero to the settlers now. They weren't praising Angus MacIvor, whose engineering skill had made the diversion possible; they applauded the glory-riding land agent who had risked flooding the whole Valley to irrigate a few fields.

French Nellie came down the alley with a sack of groceries in her arms. She smiled at Roman. "You're getting to be a stranger, Ben — spending so much time at Pilot Knob."

Roman grinned at her, marveling that Lew Gallatin's woman could be so cheerful; that any woman in her profession should retain a genuine liking for men. He said, "I have to keep watch so Lew won't sneak in another saloon on me."

French Nellie laughed. Lowering her voice to a confidential tone, she said, "I'm glad you stopped the saloon. Otherwise, Lew might've moved me to the camp."

"Well, you'd have had plenty of customers," Roman said.

"But I like Deseronto, Ben. This seems like

home to me now, and it's where I want to stay."

Walking on toward Lacey's Restaurant, Roman wondered what combination of circumstances had brought French Nellie to a house behind Lew Gallatin's tent saloon.

Lee Farnum was eating supper at Slim's counter. She said reassuringly, "Those petitions won't amount to much, Ben. I've talked to a lot of people and most of them aren't signing."

"Let them sign and be damned to them," Roman muttered. "It's no fit job, anyway."

Lee smiled at him. "It will be, when you conquer the river. You'll like the job then."

Roman shook his head. "The day we lick the Red Bull I'll put a sign on the door — 'Been here but gone.' "

"Gone where?" Lee asked.

"On a wild-horse roundup," Slim said.

"But you'll be a big man in this country, Ben," Lee said. "An important man." She studied him with lowered lids as if contemplating how he would look at some time in the future. "Imperial Development will be the most fabulous concern in the Southwest five years from now, and you'll be the man who made it so."

"I'll still take the Mogollones," Roman said. "You and Slim can have my share of fabulous Imperial Valley."

Slim went to wait on a customer, and Lee

asked, "You aren't serious, are you, Ben — about leaving here?"

Roman nodded. The expression on Lee's lamplit face now reminded him of her receptive mood during the buggy ride to the Van Horns' place. There was the same intimate tone to her voice, seductive and inviting. "There won't be any sandstorms then," he said slyly. "Just miles and miles of green fields."

She understood what he meant, and showed it in the way she smiled. At this moment she was a warm-eyed woman savoring the fine flavor of past pleasures. "Do you think there has to be a sandstorm?" she asked.

Clark Hazelhurst hurried in from the street, his face flushed and his voice high with excitement as he announced, "Southern Pacific has come in with us! They're going to build a concrete gate at Pilot Knob!"

Roman peered at him, and Lee Farnum demanded, "How do you know?"

"Phil Judson just arrived on the eastbound train. He says S.P. has put two hundred thousand dollars into the company."

"Why, that's wonderful!" Lee exclaimed. She grasped Roman's arm and shook him and demanded, "Don't you understand, Ben? The thing you said would lick the river has happened!"

Roman asked, "Where's Judson now?"

"At the saloon, waiting to buy you a drink."

As if thinking aloud, Roman mused, "Too bad John isn't here."

"But you're here!" Lee cried. "And you're the one who hung on until S.P. came in."

"John should be here," Roman said, and he was walking toward the doorway when Frank Monroe bustled into the restaurant.

"I've just talked to Judson," Monroe said, seeming dazed by what he'd heard. "Judson says you're the one who put it over. He says you talked him into applying the pressure to Epes Randolph. Is that right, Ben?"

Roman chuckled. In Monroe's eyes now was the baffled, disbelieving expression of a man fearing the collapse of profound opinions and predictions; a man wholly unprepared for disillusionment.

"Goes against the grain, doesn't it?" Roman said. Then, expanding his chest and giving Monroe an exaggerated, up-chinned appraisal, he said, "Look me over, Frank. Give yourself a treat. You're looking at the big mogul — the one you said wasn't fit to be general manager."

"But you never mentioned the fact that you had contacted Judson," Monroe protested. "You acted as if you didn't care what happened to the Valley."

"I don't," Roman said. "I'm paid for running the project — not for sweet-talking to settlers or newspaper publishers."

Roman strutted out of the restaurant, allowing the screen door to slam behind him.

Frank Monroe shook his head. As if convincing himself of a preposterous fact, he muttered, "I'll have to print it. I've criticized him when he was wrong, so I must give him credit when he's right."

"Of course you must," Lee Farnum said.

"But he's got a swelled head already," Hazelhurst said. "If you start praising him in the paper, he'll think he's God."

Monroe shrugged, bewildered as a man could be. "I can't understand why he never mentioned contacting Judson. Why should he keep such a thing secret from us all?" He took a stool at the counter, and as Slim brought him a cup of coffee, Monroe asked, "What do you think?"

"I don't know," Slim said, and absently fingered the bracelet on her wrist. "I don't know what to think, Frank."

CHAPTER TWENTY-FOUR

It was a big night for Deseronto. Men who had become conditioned to bad news converged on Gallatin's saloon with joyful eagerness. "The long wait is over!" they told each other. "We've won out at last!"

It was a big night for Ben Roman, too.

Standing at the bar with Phil Judson, he was besieged by well-wishers wanting to shake his hand. Men who had scarcely bothered to speak to him in the past now slapped him on the back and demanded the privilege of buying him drinks. There were two exceptions: Lew Gallatin, kept busy by the influx of customers, paid Roman no compliments, and Clark Hazelhurst remained sullenly aloof at one end of the bar.

Roman plied Phil Judson with questions. He learned that while Phil had quickly convinced Epes Randolph, it had taken some time to sell the proposition to the Harrimans.

Roman could scarcely believe the good news; that the thing John Chilton had dreamed of and hoped for had actually happened. He asked, "Are you sure it's all settled, Phil — that there'll be no backing out?"

"I'm positive," Judson assured him. "I've just come from San Francisco, where Epes is winding up the operating details with the Harrimans. They've put two hundred thousand dollars into Imperial Development with the provision that the money is for a concrete diversion gate at Pilot Knob. S.P. will furnish all the labor, materials, and equipment needed. You're to remain in charge until we lay track up to the intake."

Accompanying Judson to the depot, Roman asked, "How soon will you start work on the spur track, Phil?"

"Within the week. Jack Carrillo will be construction boss." Judson climbed up to a vestibule as the train began moving. He called back, "See you at Pilot Knob, Ben."

"Bueno!" Roman shouted.

He was passing the depot when the telegraph operator called from the bay window, "They've repaired the line east. I'll have some delayed weather reports after a while. Where you want 'em delivered?"

Roman thought for a moment. If he went back to the saloon he'd end up drunk. He wasn't exactly sober as it was. "I'll be at Slim Lacey's restaurant," he said, and wondered if Frank Monroe was still there.

Roman smiled, thinking of the big-mogul act he had put on for Monroe, and the gawk-eyed way Frank had looked at him. Realizing how it must have seemed to the others, Roman felt a trifle ashamed of himself. But Frank Monroe had always been so damned sure of himself, so superior in his judgments. For once Monroe had been neither critical nor self-righteous; merely bewildered. The temptation to take advantage of the unusual opportunity had been more than Roman could resist.

He was into the alley and approaching Erickson's blacksmith shop when a shadowy shape loomed out of the darkness beside him. Roman dodged as a fist grazed his chin. He swung and heard the man grunt. Then someone jumped him from behind, grasping his arms and hanging on while the first man hit him in the face.

Roman lunged sideways, dragging the man behind him. He collided with a board fence and went to his knees. Boot-churned dust got into his nostrils; the taste of blood was on his lips. He tried to get up, but a fist smashed against his jaw and he fell back on the man who held his arms.

Groggy now, Roman was aware of the smell of whisky and a bottle being forced between his lips. He swallowed until he gagged. He struggled to get up and was slugged again. Whisky choked him. He tried to pull away from the bottle, but it kept pouring whisky into his mouth.

Afterward Roman understood that he was being carried. But it didn't seem important.

Frank Monroe sat at his desk composing a front-page story for what was to be the Clarion's first "extra" edition. It was almost ten o'clock now, but men still tromped the plank walks and trade was brisk at Lew Gallatin's tent saloon.

The story should have been an easy one to write, a joyous task to accomplish. But Monroe's face, half masked by a green eyeshade, revealed the gravity of his thinking. He disliked Ben Roman as a man, and had publicly denounced him. Yet now, if Phil Judson had told the truth, Roman should be made the hero of this piece, a veritable savior of Imperial Valley.

"The big mogul," Monroe muttered, recalling Roman's brash acceptance of the role with distaste.

Clark Hazelhurst looked in through the doorway and asked, "Getting out a special edition?"

Monroe nodded. He took off the eyeshade and said, "It's an important story, Clark. A slice of history in the making." Then he asked, "How's Roman taking it?"

"Just as you'd expect. He was swilling bourbon at Gallatin's bar the last I saw of him. He should be pretty well soused by now."

Monroe sighed. He glanced at the penciled lines on the sheet of paper before him and said, "Seems odd for me to be writing him up as a hero. But I've got no choice, Clark. No matter what my personal opinion of him is, Ben Roman has accomplished the one thing that will save Imperial Valley."

"If Judson was telling the truth."

"But what reason would he have for lying about it?"

Hazelhurst shrugged. "None that I can think of," he admitted. "But I just can't see Ben Roman as a hero."

"Me neither," Monroe agreed. "An educated roustabout. A rough-and-tumble fighter who thinks might makes right and that any woman who will accept his advances is fair game. I wonder if the heroes of history were like that, Clark. Were they just glorified toughs to the thinking men who knew them?"

"They might have been," Hazelhurst said, and went on along the street.

Some time after that Slim Lacey came into the office and asked, "Do you know where Ben is?"

"At the saloon, I suppose. Why?"

"The S.P. operator brought some delayed weather reports to the restaurant. He said Ben told him to bring them there. That was an hour ago, and Ben hasn't shown up."

Monroe said, "He's probably too drunk to read a weather report. Our big mogul is celebrating tonight. He's lapping up the heady wine of public adulation."

"But these reports are important, Frank."

"Important?"

"They tell about high water. Ben should know about them at once."

Monroe got up. "I'll go fetch him," he said, and hurried across Main Street toward the tent saloon.

Slim followed him to a point across from the saloon. She visualized how it would be over there, with Ben basking in a whisky glow of praise from the crowd. Ben had never done any bragging or acted important. But he was in a bragging mood tonight.

When Monroe came out of the tent alone, she called, "Here, Frank."

He came over and said, "Ben isn't in there. Gallatin says he got awful drunk before he left. Lying-down drunk, Lew called it."

"Perhaps he went home," Slim suggested.

"I'll go look," Monroe said, and hurried off.

Walking slowly toward her restaurant, Slim thought of another place Ben might be: on the hotel veranda with Lee Farnum. She peered over there, observed a couple sitting in the shadows beyond the lamplit doorway, and thought angrily: So that's where he is!

But a moment later, as Slim came to the veranda, she saw that the man with Lee Farnum was Clark Hazelhurst. Embarrassed now, Slim said, "I thought you were Ben."

"An insult," Hazelhurst chided. Then he asked teasingly, "Is Ben late for a date?"

"No, but I wanted to tell him something. He intended to be at the restaurant an hour ago."

"This is a big night for Ben," Lee Farnum said, smiling. "We must be tolerant with him at a time like this."

Slim disliked the patronizing tone of her voice. When Lee asked, "Don't you agree?" Slim merely shrugged and watched Frank Monroe come along the sidewalk.

"He's not in his room," Frank announced.

"Why are you looking for him?" Hazelhurst asked.

"Because Slim has some delayed weather reports that Roman should see."

Hazelhurst came off the veranda at once. "Did they say anything about high water?" he demanded.

Slim nodded. "Several rivers at flood stage."

"My God!" Hazelhurst blurted. "Where are the reports?"

"At the restaurant. On the counter."

Hazelhurst started across the street at a run, then stopped and called back, "Frank, go tell Brimberry to saddle a horse for me."

"He went to Pilot Knob with a supply wagon this afternoon," Slim said, and as Monroe stood there not knowing what to do, she said urgently, "We should be looking for Ben."

"Where?" Monroe asked. "Where would we look for him?"

"Perhaps he went on the train with Judson," Lee Farnum said.

Slim shook her head. "Ben talked to the telegraph operator after the train left."

Hazelhurst came across the street. "The cut must be closed at once," he announced. "I'm taking charge at Pilot Knob and shall expect you three people to testify that it was necessary."

"But Ben must be somewhere in town," Slim protested.

Hazelhurst gave her a derisive smile. "What good is a drunken man at a time like this?"

He hurried on toward the stable with Monroe. As Slim started back along the street, Lee asked, "Where are you going?"

"To look for Ben," Slim said.

She crossed the vacant lot that ran along one side of the tent saloon and turned into the alley behind it. There was a light in Swede Erickson's lean-to room at the blacksmith shop. As she came opposite the lamplit doorway Swede peered out at her and exclaimed, "This is no fit place for you after dark! So many drunken men."

"Have you seen Ben Roman?"

Swede shook his head. "Not since he was at Gallatin's bar."

"If you see him, say that I have important news," Slim said, and went on.

"You should not be in this alley," Erickson protested.

"I'll be all right," Slim said. She passed French Nellie's place, the drawn blinds giving scarcely any illumination, and peered into the clotted shadows behind the saloon. Stacked whisky kegs gave off a sour, acrid odor here, and a man in the saloon shouted, "Hurrah for Imperial Valley, by God!"

An eastbound freight whistled far out on the flats. As Slim circled around to Main Street she heard the staccato beat of a hard-running horse. That would be Clark Hazelhurst, going to Pilot Knob. She thought: It should be Ben, and wondered where he was.

All the way back to the restaurant, Slim peered into dark places, thinking that Ben might be lying drunk somewhere along the street. Coming to a vacant lot, she crossed it twice before finally giving up and going home.

Where, she wondered, could he be?

Why hadn't anyone seen him since he left the saloon?

She was behind the counter, pouring herself a cup of coffee, when Frank Monroe came in. "Well," he said, "I've found out where Ben is."

Slim waited for him to say the rest of it; when he didn't, she asked impatiently, "Where?"

"At French Nellie's."

Slim peered at him in disbelief. She said, "No," and absently placed the coffee in front of Monroe. "He wouldn't go there, Frank. Drunk or sober."

"But he did," Monroe insisted. "I stopped by at the saloon again. Gallatin says Roman is on a bed in French Nellie's place, dead drunk."

"I don't believe it," Slim said. "Frank, you've no right to say that without being sure."

"Must I go to French Nellie's and see for myself?" he asked.

Slim said, "You've got to get him out of there."

"But why should I?"

"Because I'm asking you to, Frank."

Monroe looked at her in narrow-eyed silence for a moment. Then he said, "I've been a patient man, Slim. I've waited all this time, knowing that eventually you would see Ben Roman for what he is. If you can't see it now, you never will."

Slim shrugged. "He's what he is, Frank. Will you go get him, or must I?"

"He deserves no consideration," Monroe said. "None at all."

But as Slim came from behind the counter and walked toward the doorway, he said, "All right. I'll go get him."

There was utter resignation in Monroe's voice, and in the way he moved. All the anger faded from him. His brown eyes held the hurt, baffled expression of a man discarding a long-cherished dream. At this moment he looked old and empty and forlorn. Slim felt sorry for him. She patted his shoulder and said, "Maybe it's different from what you think, Frank."

"You mean about us?"

Slim nodded, and when his arms came around her in hesitant fashion, she gave him his kiss willingly, wishfully. He offered no protest when she drew back. His need for her was a bright shine in his eyes, but his voice was gentle as he said, "Then I'll wait some more."

Lew Gallatin stood just inside the rear doorway of his saloon and watched Frank Monroe come out of French Nellie's house with Ben Roman. The slender newspaperman supported Roman, whose knees kept buckling. He urged impatiently, "Wake up, Ben. Wake up!"

Gallatin chuckled, enjoying this. Monroe had trouble maneuvering Roman through the narrow opening in the board fence. When they got beyond the doorway's shaft of lamplight Gallatin listened to their progress along the dark alley. Roman evidently went down, for Monroe told him to get up and Roman said something about being sick. Then Swede Erickson's light went on, and presently Lew heard Monroe say, "Give me a hand with him, Swede."

Gallatin crossed the alley and smiled at French Nellie, who stood in her doorway. "The whole town will hear about it," he predicted.

"And Ben will blame me," she said worriedly. "He might make trouble for me."

Gallatin laughed at her. He said, "All you've got to do is say you found him on your doorstep, dead drunk, and put him to bed. Nobody could blame you for doing that. Folks will think you're trying to protect him. They'll think he came to you like Swede and the rest of them, but they'll give you credit for trying to protect him."

"But suppose he remembers being toted inside by —"

"He won't," Gallatin said sharply. "And you better not remember it either, hear?"

He had been idly caressing her; now he gripped a cheek between thumb and forefinger, pinching it, and his arm tightened around her waist until she gasped for breath. "You understand?" he demanded.

French Nellie nodded.

CHAPTER TWENTY-FIVE

Ben Roman understood that he was sitting at Slim Lacey's counter and that Slim was wiping his face with a towel. Presently, as she dabbed ointment on his bruised jaw, Slim asked, "Does it hurt?"

Roman shook his head. He became aware of Frank Monroe, who seemed to be leaning against him. When he pushed Monroe away, Swede Erickson came over and leaned against him. That reminded Roman of something else that had happened to him. An elusive notion kept hovering on the edge of his memory; something about two men and a bottle of whisky. . . .

"Who'd you get into a fight with?" Swede inquired.

"Fight?" Roman asked.

He was thinking about that when Slim placed a cup of coffee in front of him and said, "Drink it black, Ben."

Roman drank some of the coffee. He asked, "Was I in a fight?"

"I guess so," Slim said. "Finish your coffee."

When he gulped it down she brought him another cup and urged him to drink it.

That didn't make sense to Roman. "Why?"

"Because you're drunk," Frank Monroe said.

Roman turned to look at him. It took a long time for his eyes to focus so that he could see Monroe plainly. "The reformer," he muttered, and took a swing at Monroe, and fell off the stool.

Swede Erickson helped him up. The way Swede gripped his arms reminded Roman of something. He thought: Two men, and had a remote recollection that one of them had held his arms. He was trying to dredge up the rest of it when he heard Slim say sharply, "Please go outside, Frank."

That pleased Roman. Monroe looked comical, walking to the doorway. Like a schoolboy being sent home by his teacher. Roman grinned at Slim and took another swallow of coffee. He said, "I was in a fight."

"Who with?" she asked.

"Two men," Roman said, and tried to think who they were. Presently he said, "I don't know. But there was two of them."

It occurred to him now that Slim hadn't smiled all the time he'd been here at the counter. He asked, "You mad at me again?"

She shook her head. "Drink your coffee, Ben."

"You mad because I got drunk?" Roman asked. "Well, I didn't get drunk. That's why I didn't go back to the saloon, so I wouldn't get drunk."

After he took a few more swallows of coffee, Slim handed him a sheaf of papers. "Weather reports," she said.

Roman tried to read the top one, but the type kept blurring, and he said finally, "To hell with it."

"But there's going to be high water," Slim said. "You've got to sober up."

"Sober up?"

Slim nodded, and was holding the coffee cup for him when Lee Farnum came to the counter.

Roman pushed Swede away. He said, "Sit down, Doc," and when she accepted his invitation, Roman asked, "Do I look drunk to you?"

Lee smiled at him. She asked, "Were you in a fight?"

Roman nodded. "Two men."

He thought for a moment and said, "In the alley. That's where it was. In the alley."

Lee ordered a cup of coffee. "Have one with me," she suggested.

Roman shook his head. "No more coffee."

"But you need some more," Slim insisted.

"Quit nagging at me," Roman muttered. He grinned at Lee. "She thinks I'm drunk."

He took out his Durham sack and gave his attention to shaping a cigarette. The tobacco didn't sift into the paper properly; most of it fell onto the counter. He leaned over to see better, and managed to get a few flakes into the paper. But when he tried to roll it the paper tore apart.

Roman cursed and put the sack in his pocket. "Maybe I am drunk," he said.

Slim kept urging him to drink more coffee. He heard Lee Farnum ask Swede to go harness her horse and bring the rig to the restaurant. He asked, "Where you going, Doc?"

"To Pilot Knob," Lee said. "Want to come with me, Ben?"

Roman grinned at her. "For a drive in the moonlight?"

Lee nodded. "Might be fun."

Roman reached over to pat her shoulder, and lost his balance. Lee propped him up, and then Slim coaxed him into drinking more coffee. Afterward Lee said, "Come on, Ben."

Roman eyed her groggily. "Come where?"

"For a drive."

Roman shook his head. "I've got to stay here with Slim and drink coffee."

But Slim said, "No, Ben. You go for a drive with Miss Farnum."

That seemed odd to Roman, and so did the fact that Lee kept leaning against him as they went to the sidewalk. She had never done that before; not while they were walking. Must be in a honey-fussing mood, he thought; more so than she'd ever been. He tried to pull her around in front of him for a kiss, but she said, "Behave yourself,

Ben." Yet she kept pressing against him while they walked. It was like a square dance, sort of, like sashaying with your partner.

Roman had to make three attempts before he got into the buggy. When he reached for the reins Lee said, "I'll do the driving."

Roman slumped down in the seat and closed his eyes. He said drowsily, "A drive in the moonlight," and used Lee's shoulder for a pillow.

Swede Erickson watched the buggy go off down the dark street. He glanced at Slim, who stood in the restaurant doorway, and said, "A good idea, driving him to Pilot Knob."

Slim nodded and stood there for a moment after Swede went away. Then she went to the counter and sat on a stool and looked at the broken cigarette. She was still sitting there when Frank Monroe came to the screen door.

"May I come in now?" he asked.

Slim said, "Yes, Frank," and brushed the broken cigarette off the counter.

CHAPTER TWENTY-SIX

Roman awoke to find Lee Farnum shaking him. "We're almost to Pilot Knob, Ben."

In the time it took Roman to orient himself, she explained why they were in the buggy. "Clark read the weather reports and said MacIvor should be warned about high water. After he left town Frank Monroe and Swede Erickson brought you to the restaurant. Slim tried to sober you up with black coffee, but you were awfully drunk. And you'd been in a fight."

Roman remembered some of it now. "They jumped me in the alley," he muttered. "Two of them."

He took the reins from her and shook up the plodding horses. "What did the weather reports say?"

"Heavy rains and high water. Clark said the cut should be closed."

"The cut he insisted on," Roman muttered. He cursed, thinking that a flood now might cause Southern Pacific to withdraw from the project.

There were lights in MacIvor's office and in the cook shack, and two bonfires burned on the riverbank northeast of camp. Roman peered into the engineer's office as they passed it, seeing no one. He drove toward the cut and presently identified MacIvor and Hazelhurst among the men grouped on the collapsed dynamite dam.

Hazelhurst hurried up to the rig. "About time you got here," he said. "We'd have had a flood on our hands by now."

Roman got out of the rig and walked across the dam for a look at the river. MacIvor came over and said, "Up almost a foot in the past hour. If it keeps coming we're in for trouble."

Roman nodded. "We've got to reinforce both ends of it," he said, and called, "Mohee!"

When Brimberry came up the embankment, Roman said, "Harness every team you've got. Wagons and fresnos."

"At this time of night?" Brimberry protested.

"By morning we'd need boats," Roman said, and walked back to the rig, where Hazelhurst stood with Lee.

"Where were you sleeping it off?" Hazelhurst asked.

"Sleeping what off?"

Hazelhurst smiled at him. "Well, you weren't drinking soda pop, were you?"

"Ben got beaten up by two men in the alley," Lee said. "Can't you see the cuts on his face?"

"One held me while the other hit me," Roman said, and watched Hazelhurst's eyes. Quite sure now, he reached over and lifted the land agent's right hand and peered at the knuckles. There were no marks; no swelling. He said, "So you were the one who held me."

"What do you mean by that?" Hazelhurst demanded.

His voice sounded right. It held the proper note of bafflement. But his flame-lit face wasn't right. Apprehension altered it, and something like panic came into his eyes. He said nervously, "I don't know what you're talking about."

"Liar," Roman scoffed. He licked his bruised lips. "I'm going to show you how it feels to get slugged."

Hazelhurst backed away. He drew a pistol from his pants pocket and blurted, "I'm in charge here!"

Astonished by that announcement and the gun that accompanied it, Roman asked, "You gone loco?"

"I've taken charge and I'm telling you to get out," Hazelhurst said, and now, as Roman peered at him in squint-eyed puzzlement, the land agent snarled, "Go back to town before I kill you!"

"No, Clark! No!" Lee Farnum cried.

But Hazelhurst ignored her. Aiming the pistol at Roman, he shouted, "I should have been made general manager a long time ago. Everyone knows that!"

Roman stood perfectly still. Here, he understood, was Hazelhurst's final bid for supremacy — for the job he'd wanted so long. His sly scheming to replace Chilton had failed, but now he had one trump left. A gun trump.

"Get into that rig!" Hazelhurst ordered.

A note of frantic impatience lifted his voice to falsetto shrillness and it gave Ben Roman a thin strand of hope. Even now, with the drop on him, Hazelhurst wasn't quite sure of himself. And a man with a gun should be sure — unless he was bluffing.

Roman peered at Hazelhurst's flame-lit face, tried to evaluate what he saw there. Had hate and months of frustration driven him to the point of cold-blooded killing?

Would Hazelhurst shoot?

Or was he bluffing?

It occurred to Roman that there was only one way to find out, and that he might not live to learn the answer.

"Get into that rig or I'll shoot!" Hazelhurst said.

Roman shook his head. "I'm in charge here," he said, "and I'm staying."

Then, looking Hazelhurst in the eye, Roman walked toward him. Not quickly, not urgently, but in the leisurely way of a man stepping up to shake hands with a friend.

"Stop, or I'll shoot!" Hazelhurst warned.

Roman laughed at him. "You haven't got the nerve," he said, and loosed a gusty sigh as Hazelhurst took a step backward.

It was an odd thing, a fantastic thing for those who watched: one man, unarmed, walking toward another man who backed away with a gun in his hand.

For a hushed interval there was only the crackle of the bonfire and the soft shuffling of feet. Then, as Hazelhurst backed into the ring of watching men, Black Mike Moynihan struck his arm with a swift sledgelike fist.

In that moment, as Hazelhurst dropped the pistol, Roman lunged forward. He grasped Hazelhurst's shirt. He said, "I'm giving you twenty-four hours to leave Imperial Valley!"

Hazelhurst peered at the faces about him. He shook his head as if dazed.

"You understand?" Roman demanded, and held his right fist poised an inch from Hazelhurst's perspiring face.

The land agent nodded. He glanced briefly at Lee Farnum, and shame was naked in his eyes as he said, "I'll leave tomorrow."

Then, as Roman released his grip, Hazelhurst turned and walked toward camp.

"Ye bamboozled him!" Black Mike exclaimed.

Lee Farnum called, "Ben," and when Roman went to the rig, she demanded, "How did you know he wouldn't shoot?"

"Because he's a gentle Annie," Roman said. "No sand in his craw."

Lee shivered. "It was awful, seeing you walk toward that gun." Then she asked, "Who was the other man — the man who hit you?"

"Lew Gallatin, I think. Try to get a look at his knuckles first thing in the morning and let me know if they're bruised."

Lee nodded.

He turned to the group of gawking men and said harshly, "Show is over, boys. Now we work."

They worked all that night, rested until noon, then worked until dark. After that Roman split his force into day and night shifts to keep the barrier bolstered against a rampaging river that remained at flood tide with a constancy that drove Angus MacIvor frantic.

"It's against all reason," he complained. "This is November. Summer rains are past, and there should be no high water."

Phil Judson arrived the next morning to announce that Carrillo's track gang was setting up camp at the main line. "We'll be running ballast cars to your barrier within two weeks," he predicted.

"Better make it ten days," Roman said. "We're just barely holding it, Phil. Just barely."

Roman lost track of time. On the job all day and most of the night, he slept very little and took his meals at odd hours. He was having a snack in the cook shack one afternoon when George Frayne came in with a batch of reports that needed signing.

"Have a cup of coffee," Roman invited.

Frayne shook his head. "I must hurry right back. I've been waiting for you to return so I could get out my monthly reports and requisitions. They're way past due."

As Roman signed the papers he asked, "What's going on in town?"

Frayne didn't say anything for a moment. Then, as if reluctant to mention it, he said, "There's some talk about you. Quite a bit, in fact."

"About me being drunk?" Roman asked.

Frayne nodded, plainly embarrassed. "There was nothing in the newspaper, but it's all over town that you were found drunk on French Nellie's bed."

"No!" Roman said, more incredulous than angry. "Is that what they're saying about me?"

Frayne nodded again. "Stirred up some of the womenfolk. They're calling it a big disgrace and saying French Nellie should be run out of town."

"And me with her?" Roman asked.

"No, just her."

"Deseronto is full of damned gossips,"

Roman muttered. "I never went near French Nellie's place that night."

Then he remembered being carried. He thought: So that was it. They wanted me found in her house.

When Roman handed Frayne the papers, George asked, "Is Dr. Shumway supposed to be on the payroll?"

Roman nodded. "I forgot to tell you."

"But what will the Los Angeles office say?"

"You'll have to convince them that so big a project needs two doctors," Roman said.

"Oh, not me," Frayne objected with a fluttery fingered gesture of protest. "I couldn't possibly do that. I'm not convinced that we need another doctor."

Roman chuckled. "Well, refer them to me, then."

"I shall," Frayne said. "I certainly shall."

Watching him walk to the doorway, Roman thought: A pencil with ears. But George did a good job at the office; he was efficient and reliable. "Takes all kinds," Roman reflected.

Frayne turned and asked, "What did you say?"

"I was just thinking that this project couldn't get along without a man like you," Roman said pleasantly. "Dr. Farnum has a theory that individuals aren't important, George. But she's wrong."

"Dr. Farnum!" Frayne exclaimed, and took a sealed envelope from his hip pocket. "I almost forgot. She sent you a letter."

Roman opened the envelope. It contained a brief note, without salutation or signature: "The knuckles of Lew Gallatin's right hand appeared slightly bruised and somewhat swollen."

Frayne asked, "Any reply?"

"Just tell her thanks," Roman said.

As the chief clerk went out to his rig, Roman glanced at the note and mused, "Another score to settle."

CHAPTER TWENTY-SEVEN

The grading crew's mule-drawn scrapers were working within sight of the barrier on the fifth day. Behind them came a continuing parade of section hands shaping the roadbed, a rail-laying gang, and a horde of gandy dancers. But the river's roaring attack continued and there was no respite for hard-pressed defenders. What had been an exciting race against time degenerated into a monotonous grind; an endless ritual of rock and dirt and sandbags; a repetitious routine of sunlight and starlight, and dust that never settled.

Chocolate-brown water was washing across the barrier's south end on the morning of the eighth day.

"Give me another forty-eight hours and I'll have track on the dam," Jack Carrillo promised.

"I'll give you twenty-four," Roman bargained.

He rawhided Moynihan's fatigue-sodden men to increased effort; he enlisted the help of Carrillo's graders, and ignored MacIvor's predictions that the barrier would be breached within the hour.

It was.

Roman sensed defeat, but he refused to accept it then or later, when a second breach opened in the fill at the north end. He cursed Clark Hazelhurst, and Ronald Florsheim for listening to him. Unable to close the second breach, Roman kept it contained by bolstering the crumbling riverbank with sandbags. This sluiceway lessened the pressure at the south end. Releasing a controlled torrent of floodwater, it allowed Moynihan's crew to match each inch of the river's rise with an inch of barricade.

For a time then there seemed to be a chance of holding out until Carrillo's gang rushed rails across the dam and built a wye beyond it. But seepage caused miniature crevasses, secret tunnels no larger, at first, than the size of a man's arm. Unobserved, these small tunnels grew and merged, and, merging, grew much faster.

Both ends of the barrier went out at noon, releasing a tawny tidal wave that swept into the Alamo Canal with a thunderous roar. Men scrambled to safety on the high banks. They watched the dam dissolve and could scarcely believe what they saw.

Angus MacIvor voiced Roman's sense of futility when he shouted, "We aren't fighting just one river, Ben. We're fighting a hundred rivers."

Roman nodded. It came to him now that this roaring tumult was the combined voices of the far-off Williams, the Blue, and the Eagle. It was the Gunnison rushing out of the Sawatch Mountains, the Dolores and San Miguel off the San Juans, the Green winding down from the Wind River country with its countless creeks flowing in from the Grand Tetons and Gros Ventres. It was the hiss of the Little Snake squirming out of the Medicine Bows, the jubilant chuckling of the Yampa, the White, the San Rafael, the Dirty Devil. It was the Fremont and Escalante; the Navajo, Piedra, La Plata, Los Pinos, and Mancos; the Chaco, Gallegos, and Jalasco. All these and others were contributing to the Red Bull's roar.

Jack Carrillo peered at the rushing avalanche of muddy water and exclaimed, "What a hell of a river!"

"Can you build a trestle across it?" Roman asked.

"Not unless you can keep it from widening."

"We can," Roman said. "How long for a trestle?"

"Three weeks."

It took five, and the trestle collapsed before a rail could be layed on it.

Five weeks of repetitious failure while a continuing torrent broke through canal levees and formed a new river that gouged a broad course to the Salton Sink. Five calamitous weeks during which settlers fled from flooded farms and the citizens' committee constructed a sandbag barricade around Deseronto.

Six weeks, and then seven, while trainloads of men and material poured into Pilot Knob; while the assembled army of toilers manned steam shovels, pile drivers, and dredges, and built a roundhouse and a repair shop.

When the monthly payroll failed to arrive on time, there was a rumor that Imperial Development had gone bankrupt, and that Southern Pacific had already spent its original investment. Word came from Epes Randolph that S.P. was putting another $250,000 into the project, but Moynihan's men continued to grumble about not being paid.

Ben Roman made a hurried trip to town and demanded an explanation from George Frayne.

"It's on account of Dr. Shumway's name on the payroll," Frayne said, "and the hospital expenses. Headquarters asked for full details from you." He handed Roman a typewritten statement. "I was going to fetch it to you this evening for your signature."

While Roman signed it, George said, "Clark Hazelhurst quit his job and left a week ago."

"Good riddance," Roman muttered.

"Riley Swane is closing his hotel. He says

there won't be a town here six months from now. The Salton Sink is full of water and still spreading. Several families have moved out and others are planning to go."

"Hell with them," Roman said, and went outside.

Oscar Hoffman hailed him. "Is it true that Southern Pacific has put more money into the project?"

Roman nodded. "E. H. Harriman says he'll build a concrete gate, and he will. You can depend on that."

"By Jove, I'm glad to hear you say so!" Hoffman exclaimed. "There's been so many wild rumors, and Hazelhurst quitting like he did. . . . It's had me so worried I couldn't sleep nights." Smiling now, he grasped Roman's arm. "I'll buy you a drink," he said, and escorted Roman toward Gallatin's saloon.

Thinking of the note Lee Farnum had sent him, Roman tried to recall how long ago that had been, and was surprised that he had forgotten about it.

Lew Gallatin sat at a table, reading a newspaper. He got up now and looked at Roman and said uncertainly, "Haven't seen you around much, Ben."

Roman moved around him and stood between Gallatin and the bar before saying, "Not since that night in the alley."

"What you mean?" Gallatin asked.

"I mean you slugged me, and poured a

quart of rot-gut down my throat while Hazelhurst held me," Roman said. He glanced at Hoffman, glad that the merchant was a witness to this. Then he turned on Gallatin and hit him in the face with both fists before Lew got his hands up.

Gallatin loosed a whooshing sigh. There was no fight in him. His knees buckled and he was going down when Roman grasped his shirt.

"Not yet," Roman muttered. He clouted Gallatin with the deliberate chopping motion of a butcher swinging a meat cleaver. He said, "You stinking yellow dog!"

Then, not waiting to watch Gallatin go down, Roman turned toward the doorway.

"I think you broke his nose!" Hoffman exclaimed.

"Shouldn't wonder," Roman said.

He was on the front stoop when Hoffman called, "But I was going to buy you a drink."

"Some other time," Roman said.

Slim Lacey was washing dishes when Roman entered the restaurant. She looked at him and said, "You've lost weight, Ben."

"It's that camp cooking," Roman said. "Doesn't compare with yours."

Slim noticed his bruised knuckles. "You've been in another fight," she murmured, not censuringly or with reproof, but as if remarking about an inevitable occurrence. "I'll fix some hot salt water."

"Good girl." Soaking his hand while Slim went about her dishwashing, he said, "This is like coming home." He grinned, remembering a time long ago when he had sat in a kitchen soaking a sore hand while his mother washed dishes.

"Have you heard about Clark leaving the Valley?" Slim inquired.

Roman nodded. "That's how it always is, Slim. The ones who brag the loudest are the first to quit when the going gets rough."

"Like Dad," Slim agreed. "He was so high about the prospects here." Then she asked, "How are things at Pilot Knob?"

"Well, we're still trying to build a trestle across the break. No luck yet."

"Everyone is getting discouraged, Ben. They think there's no end to it. I've never seen folks so discouraged as they are now."

She brought his warmed-up supper to the kitchen table and watched him eat. Presently, as if expressing a fear that depressed her, she said, "I thought I'd never have to pack a valise again. This was to be my home. I don't mean this restaurant. I mean the Valley. But if the flood continues —"

"Well, you could go on that mustang gather with Mohee Jim and me," Roman suggested. "We'd be real glad to have a good cook along."

Slim wasn't amused. She asked soberly,

"Aren't you ever going to settle down?"

"Sure, but it won't be in a town, or on a farm," Roman said. "I'll have a little cow outfit in a big country." Thinking of what Brimberry had said, he added, "Where there's room enough and time enough."

Afterward, when he was leaving, Roman tweaked her chin and said, "Don't let them discourage you, Slim. Maybe you won't have to pack your valise."

But that didn't seem to please her, and she didn't smile as she watched him go.

Five families whose places were under water were camped in a fallow field behind the Borgstrom barn. Sleeping in wagons or on the ground, they had waited patiently for the flood to end; now, as they sat around a common supper fire, they listened to Joe Grimshaw, who was pulling out of the Valley in the morning.

"I say we been played for a passel of fools," the big Kansan said, voicing a futility that nagged them all. "We was tolled here by big brags and promises. The garden spot of America, Clark Hazelhurst called it — a land of milk and honey. But it's turned out to be flood and mud. Where's Hazelhurst now? Gone, by God — run off like a rat desertin' a sinkin' ship And that's what this damned Valley is. A sinkin' ship!"

Doc Shumway, returning from a call to

Lateral 20, heard Grimshaw's talk as he drove into the yard. He waved a greeting to Karen, who called from the lamplit kitchen, "Supper's ready, Doctor."

Shumway smiled. He had suggested that Karen call him John, now that they were husband and wife, but she seldom did when others were around. Even in Jan's presence it was "Doctor." But at night, in the privacy of their bedroom, she called him John. . . .

As he unhitched and fed the horse, Doc heard Grimshaw demand bitterly, "What's the sense in stayin' until we starve to death?"

Someone, it sounded like Gus Elmendorf, said, "We own land here. We've got to stay."

"You own a mudhole," Grimshaw retorted. "A typhoid-fever mudhole that has cost the life of your little girl!"

Doc walked over to the fire and asked quietly, "Where do you propose to go?"

"Back to Kansas, by God. Back where I came from."

"There has been typhoid fever in Kansas," Doc said. "There have been drought and flood and hard times."

He glanced at Hattie Elmendorf, who would soon have a baby to take the place of little Agnes. He said, "It's not the company's fault that there are floods."

"But it's their fault for not buildin' a proper intake gate," Grimshaw insisted.

Doc shook his head. He considered the

flame-lit faces of men whose hope had worn thin, observing some who had no hope at all. He thought: I was like that for a long time. Without hope.

"Whose fault is it, then?" Grimshaw demanded.

"The bureaucrats in Washington who ruined Imperial's financial standing with such slanderous announcements," Doc said. "That's why there wasn't enough money to construct a proper intake gate. But now, with Southern Pacific in the company, there'll be one."

Gus Elmendorf asked, "Do you think they'll close the break and stop future floods?"

"I do," Doc said. "It may take a little more time, but they will do it. I'm sure of that."

Afterward, eating supper with Karen, he said hopefully, "Some of them will go with Grimshaw tomorrow. But some will stay."

CHAPTER TWENTY-EIGHT

All through November and December and January the struggle at the break continued while bitter-eyed men toiled on trestles that were washed away. Los Angeles newspapers predicted that Imperial Valley would become an inland sea. Crews worked around the clock, with Carrillo, MacIvor, and Phil Judson devising new methods of attack.

It was the first week of February when Carrillo's gang laid rail over a completed trestle. On that day, as the first ballast cars crossed the creaking span, a great shout went up from the assembled workers. But presently, as a train-load of rock cascaded into water and disappeared, the cheering died down. A second trainload was dumped, without visible effect; a third and a fourth.

"A bottomless pit," MacIvor muttered.

And Carrillo demanded, "Where's all the rock going — to China?"

But Roman said confidently, "You'll find bottom if you keep the rock coming."

It kept coming, day after day, while Southern Pacific's crack passenger trains were delayed on sidings and E. H. Harriman commanded, "Close that break at all costs!"

Epes Randolph arrived in his private car with Ronald Florsheim and three newspaper reporters as his guests. The group watched laboring locomotives drag ballast cars onto the trestle, listened to Carrillo's report of daily tonnage.

Two thousand carloads of rock had been dumped before the barricade rose above swirling brown water; it took another four hundred carloads of gravel and clay to seal the gigantic barrier. On February tenth, it was done.

There was no cheering at Pilot Knob that day.

Men peered at the dry barricade without moving or speaking. Tired men who leaned on shovels, or sat on fresnos, or stood in shoulder-slumped weariness. Silent, solemn-faced men like Black Mike Moynihan, who understood that he was seeing the end of a big thing. A monstrous thing.

Ben Roman stood beside Angus MacIvor and said quietly, "John should be seeing this."

"I didn't believe it would ever happen," MacIvor muttered with the reluctance of a born pessimist. "There's the foundation for a concrete gate."

Mohee Jim came up to Roman. He said, "The Red Bull is licked. Are we through with this outfit now?"

Roman nodded.

"Then let's hit a shuck for town," Mohee Jim said eagerly.

"Soon as I tell Florsheim," Roman said.

Imperial's president couldn't understand his resignation. "But why quit now, when all the hard work is done?" Florsheim demanded.

"I don't like office work," Roman explained. "And I've got another proposition that looks good to me."

As Florsheim shook his head and wished him well, Roman said, "I hope you'll keep Doc Shumway on as a second doctor. The project needs him."

"Miss Farnum convinced me of that in Deseronto yesterday," Florsheim said. He chuckled, adding, "She also convinced me that we'll soon be needing a larger, better equipped hospital."

Roman was thinking about that as he rode out of Pilot Knob with Brimberry. He said with amusement, "She's a doer, Mohee — a natural-born doer."

"Who?"

"The lady doctor."

Brimberry eyed him suspiciously. "You ain't thinkin' of marryin' her, be you, Ben?"

Roman shook his head. "She's already married."

"Who to?"

"A hospital," Roman said.

Mohee Jim spat tobacco juice. He said disgustedly, "That don't mean she wouldn't marry a man."

"Suppose not, Roman agreed. "But who wants to play second fiddle to a hospital?"

"Or to a restaurant, either," Brimberry said.

Roman thought about that for a moment. Mohee Jim asked impatiently, "Ain't that right, Ben?"

"Well, the restaurant doesn't mean much to Slim. It's just a way of making a living. She'd sooner be in her own home, I reckon. But she wants to stay put where she is. She's had her fill of traveling."

As they approached town, Brimberry asked, "How about us takin' the night train east?"

Roman nodded. It was sundown now, and a cool breeze stirred dust on the flats. He said, "A trifle early in the season for a trip into the Mogollones, though. Still winter up there."

"Won't make no difference at all," Mohee Jim said. "We can track them mustangs down in the snow, and corral 'em easier."

"Suppose," Roman said.

But he wasn't thinking about mustangs when he walked into Lee Farnum's office a few minutes later; he was remembering how it had been that night on the way to the Van Horns' place.

Glancing about the neat lamplit office, Roman said, "All painted white, just like you wanted."

Lee got up from her desk and asked eagerly, "Is it finished, Ben? Have you closed the break at last?"

Roman nodded.

"Oh, that's wonderful!" she exclaimed. "Simply wonderful!"

She hurried to him, smiling and excited. "You've done it!" she cried. "You've conquered the river!"

"Well, with considerable help," Roman said. "It wasn't exactly a one-man deal."

"But you were the one who kept it going — the one who refused to quit," Lee insisted, frank admiration in her glowing eyes. "Now you can stay in town and be the biggest man for miles around!"

Roman shook his head.

"Why not?" Lee demanded.

"I resigned this afternoon."

"You resigned!" she exclaimed. "Oh, Ben, you're just joshing me. You don't really mean that."

"Sure I mean it. I told you how it would be, a long time ago. I'm through."

Lee stared at him, her disbelief changing to anger. "Do you mean to say you've quit Imperial Development to go on a crazy roundup with Mohee Jim?"

She looked now as she had that first day in his office; the day she had called him an idiot. Anger warmed her eyes and stained her cheeks as she demanded, "Why can't you be like other men?"

Roman shrugged. Then he grinned at her and asked, "Why can't you be like other women?"

That question had its instant effect on her; it altered the tone of her voice as she sighed, "I'm a doctor and you're a —"

Roman waited before asking, "An idiot?"

She shook her head. "A drifter."

Then in a resigned voice she asked, "When are you leaving?"

"Tonight."

"So soon? Why all the rush?"

"No reason for staying."

Lee moved close to him. She placed her hands on his shoulders and asked softly, "Are you sure about that, Ben? Are you sure there's nothing for you here?"

It was an invitation too plain for him to miss or to ignore. It stirred old impulses in Roman; it disrupted the orderly run of his thoughts so that he wasn't quite sure of past impressions. But he said soberly, "I don't know how to explain it, Lee. Some men like towns and office jobs. But some don't, and nothing can change that."

"Not even a woman?" she asked, pressing close to him.

Roman shook his head.

She moved back then and turned away from him, more subdued than he had ever seen her, and more listless. It was as if she had offered him all there was to offer and had nothing left to say. Presently she asked, "Is Slim Lacey going with you?"

That startled Roman. "Of course not," he said. "Why ask such a foolish question?"

Lee shrugged and went back to her desk. She sat down and looked at him impersonally. "Well, I've got this hospital, thanks to you."

"And Ronald Florsheim says you'll soon have a much better one," Roman said.

"Did he tell you that?" she asked, immediately brightening. "Do you think he really means it?"

Roman nodded, and in this moment understood what he had long suspected: that no man could arouse Lee Farnum as a hospital could. It was in her eyes now, plain for him to see, and in her voice when she murmured, "A large, well-equipped hospital with a competent staff."

Roman turned to the doorway. He said quietly, "All painted white," and going out, wondered if she was aware of his departure.

Main Street was quiet at this hour. Wood smoke from supper fires made a pleasant aroma and lamplit windows fashioned cheerful beacons against the dusk. Thinking back to all the times he had tromped this plank walk toward Lacey's Restaurant, Roman thought: The last time, and wondered why Deseronto seemed like a pleasant place this evening; why it was no longer a trap from which he needed to escape. Then the answer came to him and he thought: Because I'm leaving it.

Mohee Jim was among the half-dozen customers at Slim's counter. As Roman came in he heard Brimberry say, "We're leavin' on the night train and we won't be back."

Swede Erickson got up from a stool beside Mohee Jim. "Take this seat," he said. "I'm through eating." Then the blacksmith asked, "Is it true, what Mohee says about you leaving?"

"Finished my job," Roman said, and now, as Slim came to take his order, he asked teasingly, "Are you the one they call Big Slim?"

She regarded him soberly. "You look awful."

Roman thumbed his jaw. Remembering another time she had looked at him like this, he asked, "Are my eyes like burned holes in a blanket?"

"You're thin as a rail," Slim said. "You look as if you'd been dragged through a knothole."

Not a word about the big news. No praise for the long, tough battle he had waged against the river. Comparing this with Lee Farnum's enthusiastic reception, Roman marveled that two women could be so different in every way.

"I'll fix you a T-bone steak," Slim said, and went into the kitchen.

Roman winked at Brimberry. "That's how I rate in this town. T-bone steaks on the house."

"That's nothin' to brag about," Brimberry said. "She gave me two of 'em free gratis for trailin' you into a sandstorm."

Roman eyed him thoughtfully. "Did Slim ask you to follow me that day?"

"Ask, hell. She pushed me out of the door bodily. Wouldn't even let me take time to eat first, by God."

Roman thought about that as Mohee Jim finished his supper. It occurred to him that Slim had also been involved the night Clark Hazelhurst knocked him out with a chair, and again when he'd been slugged in the alley. He had wondered how it happened that Frank Monroe found him that night and took the trouble to bring him here. Now Roman thought: Slim sent him to look for me.

It occurred to him that Slim was a doer, too. She didn't make much fuss about the things she did, but she got the job done. Unlike Lee, Slim believed in doing things for individuals. She wasn't much concerned with people generally, but she'd do things for a person.

Brimberry placed fifty cents beside his plate. He said, "I'll go pack my stuff. We ain't got much time." His face wore an exuberant smile and there was a swagger in the way he walked. "I'll tote your saddle to the depot and check it along with mine," he announced on his way out.

The steak Slim prepared was delicious. "Best I ever ate," Roman told her.

The last customer had gone when he finished his pie. He was on the point of accepting a second piece when he looked at the clock and announced, "I've got to go pack my war sack."

Slim walked to the doorway with him, saying, "I hope you have good luck on the roundup."

"Well, we may not get rich, but it'll be a change," Roman said.

He stood on the stoop with her, not knowing how to say good-by to this sober-faced girl who stood so quietly waiting.

"Any chance of your changing your mind?" he asked.

"About what?"

"Leaving Imperial Valley."

She studied his face while she thought about it. Presently she asked, "With you?"

Roman nodded.

She kept looking at him, studying him. "You're like Dad, always wanting to go somewhere. You'd never stay put, even on a ranch."

"And so you'll marry the reformer," Roman said, wanting it to sound casual and not sure that it did.

"Frank is a fine man," Slim said. "And he'll stay put." She sounded half angry now. "I'll not live like my mother did, pillar to post, and never having a real home of my own."

She opened the screen door and turned and stood there, more agitated at this moment than he'd ever seen her, and somehow more beautiful. "Don't gawk at me," she cried as if at her wits' end. "Go on your darned roundup and don't ever come back!"

Then she went inside, allowing the door to slam behind her.

The eastbound train was whistling its distant signal when Roman walked down Main Street with his duffel bag balanced on a shoulder. Lamplight made a yellow shine in front of Hoffman's Mercantile, and Roman thought: Must be Saturday night. It occurred to him now that the days of the week hadn't meant anything at Pilot Knob for a long time.

Doc Shumway came off the stoop with a sack of flour. He placed it in a wagon at the hitch rack and turned to Roman, asking, "What's this I hear about you leaving the Valley?"

"Tonight," Roman said, and tipped his hat to Karen, who came out now with a basket of groceries.

"We were going to the depot to see you off," she said.

Doc shook hands with Roman. "You've done what John Chilton wanted, and now you're free." His lamplit eyes twinkled; he smiled, thinking back. "Remember our talk about being trapped, Ben? Now we are both free."

Roman thought about that as he walked to the depot. For the first time in months there was no bond of allegiance to hold him, no sense of loyalty to detain him. He was free. But he felt no exuberance, and he understood that it was because of Slim Lacey. Recalling her agitation, he felt a nagging regret, and resented it. A footloose man shouldn't worry about a woman who wanted to remain in one place all her life. It wasn't his fault that she'd never had a home.

The train came in as Roman reached the platform. Mohee Jim said impatiently, "Begun to think you wasn't comin'. I got our tickets."

Roman tossed his duffel sack into the vestibule. He peered across the darkness to Main Street's lamplit windows and said, "Been here but gone."

"Well, you don't sound very glad about it," Brimberry said. "Ain't you happy to be leavin' this place?"

Roman identified the hospital's lighted windows and thought: She's got what she really wanted. He couldn't see Lacey's Restaurant from here, but he thought: So has Slim.

The engine tooted two sharp blasts now, and Mohee Jim said exultantly, "Here we go, Ben! Here we go!"

Roman was following him up the steps when he heard a woman call frantically, "Ben. Wait for me!"

Turning, he saw her run across the dark platform with a valise in one hand and a coat in the other. He leaned out and got an arm around her and hauled her up.

Slim put down the valise. Color stained her cheeks, and rapid breathing disturbed the pleated bodice of her blouse. Roman watched her tuck back a strand of windblown hair. He asked wonderingly, "Where you going?"

Slim shrugged. "With you, Ben. Wherever you go."

Roman took her in his arms. He tilted her face so he could look into her eyes. "Are you sure you want to, Slim?"

"Sure," she whispered.

Roman kissed her in the gentle way of a man humbled by a precious and unexpected gift. But presently, with her womanly warmth and fragrance having its way with him, he brought her yielding body hard against his own. He was still kissing her when Mohee Jim came out to the vestibule and demanded, "What's goin' on?"

"We're practicing for our marriage in

Tucson," Roman announced.

"Marriage? What about me?"

"Why, you'll be best man," Roman said, and went on with his practicing.